Treasures by the Sea

Treasures by the Sea

Sally Streib

Pacific Press Publishing Association
Boise, Idaho
Oshawa, Ontario, Canada

Edited by Lincoln Steed
Designed by Tim Larson
Cover by Barbara Steadman
Typeset in 10/12 Century Schoolbook

Library of Congress Catalog Card Number: 90-62274

ISBN 0-8163-0933-7

91 92 93 94 95 • 5 4 3 2 1

Contents

Topic   Page

Not Just an Interesting Story

Treasures by the Sea has all the ingredients that make up a great-reading story for the younger set. By the time you make chapter 26, Eric and Susan will be best friends, and their exciting adventures will be yours too. But the pluses go way beyond that level. Author Sally Streib has used the story to introduce you to all the major beliefs of the Seventh-day Adventist Church—in the most easy-to-understand manner.

1
Storm Clouds

Eric stood near the bedroom window and gazed at the dark clouds rolling across the sky like tumbleweeds driven over a prairie by a great wind. The clouds soon piled up into heaps until they blotted out the afternoon sun. Crooked fingers of lightning reached into the darkness, revealing for an instant the churning gray waters of Chesapeake Bay. The summer storm raged against the land like the troubled thoughts that churned inside Eric's mind. All at once the clouds burst open, and giant raindrops pounded against the window.

"Eric! Eric! Are you there? May I come in?"

"Come on in." Eric never turned from the window. He brushed a stray tear from his cheek and struggled to gain control of his voice.

The door flew open and Susan burst inside. She stood shivering in the darkened room.

"Are you afraid too?" she asked.

"Of course not," Eric blurted. "I was just sitting here thinking, that's all."

"I'm scared," Susan said. She still hadn't moved from the doorway. Another rumble of thunder made her shake even harder.

Eric pulled the curtains together to shut out the

storm. He flopped down on the rug beside his bed. "You can stay here if you want," he said, motioning for Susan to join him. "It's a pretty bad storm."

Susan inched closer. "I hate storms. I feel so scared. I seem to be afraid of everything now that Mother's gone. What's going to happen to us, Eric?"

"I don't know. But you know Dad is trying to work something out." He reached over and gave Susan an awkward pat on her shoulder.

"I—I wish I could be brave like you are, Eric," Susan sobbed. "Don't you ever feel afraid or sad?" She looked up at him.

He knew it would be hard to lie to his twin sister. He just couldn't tell her how he felt. Maybe she wouldn't understand just how angry and confused he felt. "I don't want to go away, that's all," he said, banging a clenched fist into the rug.

"Can't you talk to Dad?"

"That's easy for you to say. You can talk to anyone about what you think. Besides, Dad wouldn't understand."

"Eric! Susan! Where are you?"

"It's Dad!" Eric jumped up and opened the door. "We're in here, Dad."

Dad's head appeared around the doorway. "Hey, what are you doing sitting in the dark?"

"Oh, I was just watching the storm. Susan was scared, so I pulled the curtains."

"We were talking, Dad," Susan added.

"I see." Dad sat down on the bed. "Looks pretty gloomy to me. Something you want to share with me?"

Susan gave Eric a this-is-your-chance-to-talk-to-him glance. Eric noticed the tired look in his father's eyes, how his face seemed so dull and lifeless. *Oh, why did*

Mother have to die? he thought. *Why did that old drunk have to hit her? I hate him, I hate him! Now my whole life is ruined. Torn up!* His thoughts crowded out the words he wanted to say.

"We don't want to be sent away, Dad," Susan almost shouted.

"So that's it." He pulled his daughter close. "I know this isn't how any of us want it. But for now, it's the best I can manage. Your Aunt Myrtle has agreed for you to stay with her for the next school year until—"

"A whole year!" Eric blurted. "But Dad—"

"I know, Eric. There's the baseball team. You won't be able to play this year. And all your friends. I know you'll miss them. But I have a big problem. I have to sell the house and finish my last year at the university. I just don't know how I can handle all this." He leaned forward, resting his head in his hands. The room filled up with silence.

"We can help," Susan began in a small voice. "I can cook and clean the house, and Eric—"

"Susan!" Dad said in a strong voice. "You and Eric are only twelve. When I sell the house, where will we live? No, that's final. I don't like this either, but for your sakes it's best. Aunt Myrtle is a good woman. She has a lovely home on the ocean, so you'll have everything you need there."

Eric was surprised to hear himself say, "We don't want everything. We want you, Dad!"

Susan caught her breath. Eric had said what they had both been so afraid to say. No one spoke for a long moment.

"I see," Dad said at last. "You're afraid you'll lose me too." He looked at Susan and Eric for several long moments. "Do you two think for one moment that . . . ?"

Susan ran to her father and buried her head on his shoulder. Eric pressed against his other side, and the three clung together in the darkened room.

"I just don't know what else I can do," Dad said in a quiet voice. "You do understand, don't you?" his voice pleaded.

"Sure, Dad." Eric nudged Susan.

"Yes, Dad. We'll be all right," Susan whispered, her voice quivering.

"Now, let's make the best of this." Dad stood up and started for the door. "Why don't you wash up for supper?"

The door shut, and Eric looked at Susan. "A lot of good it did to talk to Dad," he grumbled.

"Maybe there just isn't anything else he can do," Susan reasoned. "We could try to understand."

"Sure," Eric said, his voice heavy with doubt.

The next two days passed by slowly. A silent gloom settled over the house. Eric spent most of the day in his room, brooding. Dad kept busy at the office. Susan spent hours wandering along the edge of the bay. She dug her toes into the golden sand or watched the sailboats skim over the water. How she would miss the bay! Everything good and familiar seemed to have drained out of her life. Would she ever be happy again? Would Eric? She missed his carefree moods and his teasing. He didn't laugh anymore. And he was always so grumpy. If only she could talk to Mother right now.

"How can I do without her?" She spoke to a sea gull that swooped down beside her. He plunged his bill into the wet sand, then flew out over the bay.

"I wish I could just fly away like you," Susan called. She scanned the sky after him. *How high can a gull fly? What's beyond the clouds, anyway? Does God live there somewhere? Mother used to say, "Susan, God wants the best for us, no matter how hard it seems at times."*

Another gull circled overhead, then landed on the water. His body bobbed over the gentle swells.

Susan cupped her hands around her mouth. "Hey, old sea gull, who made you?" she yelled.

The gull just floated along, not seeming to care.

Oh, well, Susan thought, *even if there is a God who created everything, I don't know if I want to know Him. He let Mother die in that terrible accident, didn't He? Still . . .*

"I'll just ask Aunt Myrtle," she decided aloud.

"Do you always talk to the gulls?" Eric said, coming up behind her.

Susan jumped! "Do you have to scare a person?"

"Come on. Dad's home early and wants to talk to us."

The twins walked silently up the beach and opened the back door to the kitchen. Dad leaned against the cupboard, sipping a hot drink.

"Hi," he said. A small smile played at the corners of his mouth. "Sit down, and let's eat."

Susan gazed in amazement at the supper table. Potatoes, a roast, and salad sat in the middle of the table. Three places had been neatly set, and even a flower poked a brave head from a small vase at the end of the table.

"You did all this?" she gasped.

"I certainly did," Dad said proudly, wiping his hands on a towel. "We're going to celebrate."

"Celebrate! But why?" Eric blurted.

"Because I have news," Dad said smugly. "It can wait until we eat, however."

"No, Dad. Tell us now, or I won't be able to eat a bite," Susan shouted, tugging on her father's arm.

"Impossible, impatient woman!" Dad teased. "Well, sit down, then. You see, I've worked something out with my boss and also with the university."

"OK! Wow!" Eric almost exploded with enthusiasm.

"Not so fast, son." A firm tone crept into Dad's voice, and his smile faded a bit. "First of all, I plan to train my partner, Bill Hays, to take over my job for a year. Second, if I take the summer session at the university and work with the extension program next fall, I can still graduate a year from now. I'll have to return there for tests and for another class or two. By next fall we should be able to return together and find a home that suits us."

"But we still have to stay with Aunt Myrtle this summer." Susan's voice was flat. She twisted her long brown braids together.

"That's true, princess. At the end of the summer, I'll join you both in California, and we'll be together again."

Susan flung her arms around Dad's neck. "That's what we want most," she cried, "to be together."

"I know that now." Dad rumpled her bangs with his large hand.

"Well, son, do you think you can live with that?"

"Sure, Dad!" Eric felt disappointment fill his mind. Yet, three months seemed better than a whole year. Still, the whole thing made him uneasy. He didn't want to live in California anyway, much less with a spinster aunt he didn't even know.

The next two weeks were filled with activity. The house fairly shone. Eric cleaned all the windows himself. Almost before they knew it, their treasures and clothing were packed, and a jet carried them across the country and settled with a jerk on the runway in Ontario, California.

"Do you think we will be able to recognize Aunt

Myrtle from the picture Dad gave us?" Susan asked anxiously as she tugged at the small suitcase.

"How should I know?" Eric retorted. "With all these people, I don't even know where I am going."

"Let's just stand here and let her find us," said Susan.

"Hello, hello, there!" a cheerful voice called out over the noise of the crowded room. "Eric? Susan?"

A rather small woman weaved her way through the crowd. Her dancing blue eyes peeped from under a straw hat. She wore a pink flowered dress that made her cheeks look pink too. Eric and Susan just stared.

"Aunt Myrtle?" Eric said hesitantly.

"Young man, you've really grown up, haven't you? And Susan! You look just like your mother." Her eyes looked sad for a moment; then she smiled and motioned for them to follow her.

At last they located their baggage and then rode along the streets toward the place that would be their new home.

Later, Aunt Myrtle showed them to a room with twin beds. "I thought you might like to share a room for this one night. It isn't easy to be in a new place. I have several empty rooms, and tomorrow you can choose which one you wish to have. How does that sound?"

"Fine. Thank you, ma'am," said Eric.

"Aunt Myrtle, Dad said there were lots of rocks by the sea and that you'd show us things that live there."

"That's right, Susan. You see, I used to be a very unhappy woman. I guess those sea creatures taught me a lot. How to think differently, you might say."

Eric felt too tired to think about anything. He pulled the quilt up around his neck and soon fell sleep. Susan's head danced with questions. Those sea creatures might teach her something interesting. Maybe about God.

2

Aunt Myrtle's Cliffs

W hen are you two sleepyheads going to wake up?" Aunt Myrtle's voice broke into the quiet morning. She stood in the open doorway of the twins' room and smiled.

Eric peeked out from under the quilt, then ducked under the covers and groaned. Susan sat up with a jerk and stretched.

"Want to go for an early-morning walk?" Aunt Myrtle invited. "The tide is out, and there just might be one of those creatures I told you about last evening."

"Sure!" Susan jumped out of bed. "Come on, Eric!"

"You'll have to hurry a bit, then," Aunt Myrtle said. "This is the best time to discover things. I'll meet you in the kitchen in ten minutes." She turned and was gone.

Susan threw a pillow at the mound in the bed across the room. "Get up, lazy," she called. "I want to see what it's like around here."

"Do you have to discover the whole world right now?" Eric moaned. "Give me a break. No school and I can sleep in. Go away!"

"I'm not going without you, so come on," Susan persisted, pulling the covers off Eric's bed.

In less than twenty minutes Eric and Susan found themselves following Aunt Myrtle down the still-cool

16

sand toward the seashore.

"Look at that!" Eric shouted over the noise of waves crashing on the shore.

A giant mound of greenish water began to build up like a great wall. For an instant it hovered, then crashed down toward the beach, sending foam and bubbles into the air.

Eric could hardly believe his eyes.

"Let's climb up the cliff and see what we can find," Aunt Myrtle called to the twins, who stood staring at the waves before them.

Eric noticed his aunt for the first time that day. She wore old tennis shoes with holes in the toes. Her white slacks were rolled up to the knees, and her hair was tied back in a ponytail. She carried a green canvas pack on her back. Aunt Myrtle certainly seemed to enjoy life.

Eric and Susan picked their way up over the rocky surface of the cliff.

"Watch that green seaweed. It makes the rocks slippery," Aunt Myrtle instructed just as Eric's foot flew out from under him and he sat down hard on a wet rock. Susan swallowed a laugh that threatened to burst out.

Aunt Myrtle groped around in a deep pool of water. She parted the strands of seaweed and felt along the surface of the rocks.

"I've got one," she shouted.

Eric and Susan crept closer and peered into the pool. Aunt Myrtle slipped a knife blade under the edge of a disklike shell that was clasped to the rock. It popped off and landed at Eric's feet.

"It sure is ugly," Eric grumbled, picking up the shell and poking the gray blob of flesh that he felt sure must be the creature which lived inside. He turned the shell over. The outside looked just like a plain chunk of rock.

17

Several tiny barnacles clung to the rough surface.

"Let's take a closer look," Aunt Myrtle suggested. She took the shell and scooped out the animal. It had no shape at all—it looked like a great suction cup.

"This can cling to the rocks very well," Aunt Myrtle explained. "Can you imagine the tons of water that crash against these cliffs every time a wave hits? The dome shape of the shell keeps it from being washed away into the sea. But there is an even more wonderful thing about the abalone shell. Take a look inside."

Susan took the shell in her hands and looked at the now-exposed inner side. A shaft of morning light reflected off the shell. "It's beautiful!" she exclaimed.

"Wow!" Eric said. "It really is something."

Susan noticed that the frown seemed to have fallen off his face for a moment, at least. "Did that ugly animal make all the color of this shell?" Eric asked.

"It certainly did, Eric." Aunt Myrtle smiled. "Now sit down and I'll tell you why this creature helped me understand God's love."

"At first glance this shell seems of so little beauty and value," Aunt Myrtle began. "But when you look inside you see the beautiful patterns of color the creature created. So many times I've looked at myself and said, 'You are so plain. You are not very special.' But you see, when God looks at me, He does not say that at all. He sees that I am like this abalone shell. With His power I can create something beautiful with my life. Actually, God is the One who does it for me after I give Him permission to take control of my life."

"Aunt Myrtle," Susan said, "the abalone clings to the rocks and isn't swept out to the sea when those waves crash against them. I remember Mother saying once that God is like a strong rock. She said that I would always be safe if I stayed close to Him."

"Perhaps, Susan, it is easier to understand things when you can see them. I think that's why God gave us the things in nature. They help us to know what God is like. When we see that He's a God of love and has made us special, we want to know Him better."

"Well, how do you know for sure there is a God who made all these things?" Eric objected.

"To be honest, Eric, I can't prove it absolutely. But when I see the complicated and lovely things in nature, and I read what my 'Operator's Manual' says, it seems easy to believe."

"Operator's manual! What's that?" Susan asked.

"An operator's manual is a book that comes with anything you buy. Like a car or something," Eric said, making a face at Susan.

"That's exactly right, Eric." Aunt Myrtle laughed. "And God made me. He gave me a very good Guide to help me know the best way to live and to know Him, the Creator. Look! I have my own Manual with me." She reached into her pack and pulled out a small green book. "To answer your question, Eric, right here in the first book of this Guide you find God telling just how He created the beauty you see before you. Here it is, the first chapter of Genesis. 'In the beginning God created the heavens and the earth' " (Genesis 1:1).* Aunt Myrtle continued to read the entire story of the earth's creation. " 'And God saw all that He had made, and behold, it was very good,' " she finished.

The twins sat silently looking out over the sea. Eric turned the shell over and over in his hands.

"Just imagine this for a minute," Aunt Myrtle con-

---

*Bible texts in this chapter are from the New American Standard Bible.

tinued. "In the book of Isaiah God says it this way. 'It is I who made the earth, and created man upon it. I stretched out the heavens with My hands' " (Isaiah 45:12).

Eric stood up and spread his hands out. "Let there be the sea and abalone shells . . ."

"What are you doing?" Susan demanded.

"I was just imagining how God—never mind," Eric said, sitting down and handing the shell to Aunt Myrtle.

"Aunt Myrtle," Susan said, twisting her braids together, "even if God did create me special and all that, well—how do you know He really loves me?"

"Because, Susan, it says so right here in my Operator's Manual, the Bible." She turned the pages, stopping at the book called 1 John. "John, one of God's friends, wrote this. 'See how great a love the Father has bestowed upon us, that we should be called the children of God' (1 John 3:1). So you see, God loves me and He loves you. He wants us to be His children."

"And," Susan said, "He wants us to stay close to Him like the abalone shell does to the cliff."

"Yes. Then even waves of trouble can't wash us away once we learn to trust Him," Aunt Myrtle said, dropping the abalone shell into a plastic bag.

Eric jumped up. "Say, let's get going. Isn't this the day we get to choose our own room?"

A wave splashed close to their spot on the rocks, and they scrambled away like crabs over the cliff.

Eric could hardly wait to ask Aunt Myrtle about a small room he'd noticed when snooping about the house that first evening. It had a window overlooking the sea, and it sat alone at one end of the upper floor of the house. Aunt Myrtle seemed to understand a lot of things. Did she understand how much he needed a place with some privacy. A place to think?

3

Celebration Day

"Yes, Eric, I suppose you can use the observation room. But why have you chosen it? There are other rooms that would give you so much more space to spread out your things." Aunt Myrtle gave the room an appraising look.

"I don't know, ma'am." Eric jammed his hands into his jeans pockets and stared at his tennis shoes.

"All right," Aunt Myrtle agreed. "But the room is quite full of things that will need to be moved to the storage shed. Are you willing to do that?"

"Sure thing, ma'am!" Eric was already arranging boxes in the small room.

"Eric, wait!"

"Yes, ma'am?"

"Will you kindly do me the favor of calling me Aunt Myrtle? 'Ma'am' makes me feel rather old. Can't say as anyone ever called me that before." She smiled.

"OK, Aunt Myrtle. You really don't look like a ma'am to me anyway," he said, remembering the clothes she had worn on their morning walk. He gave her a quick grin, turned, and fled down the stairs.

"He smiled!" Susan exclaimed, coming up behind Aunt Myrtle.

"Ever so slightly," Aunt Myrtle said. "Now, Susan,

what room have you chosen?"

"I'd like the large room just at the head of the stairs." Susan hugged herself. "There's a great view of the garden from the window seat. Could we put fluffy white curtains at the window? They would go so nicely with the new bedspread Father bought for me just before we left."

"Hold on a minute!" Aunt Myrtle covered her ears in mock despair. "Not so many questions. It always seems that you want to say everything at once, Susan." Aunt Myrtle laughed.

Susan noticed that Aunt Myrtle laughed a lot. She decided that was a very nice thing about this woman she now called aunt.

"I will ask Eric to carry your things up. When you have them arranged, let me know. I have just the curtains for that window."

Hours later, the twins were still busy in their new rooms.

"Children, are you settled enough to come and give me some help?" Aunt Myrtle called up the stairs. "It's time I got things ready for the Sabbath."

"Sabbath?" Eric whispered as he met Susan in the hall. "What does she mean?"

"I don't know, Eric. I do remember Dad saying something about Aunt Myrtle having some different ideas about religion, and that we must respect them since we are guests of a sort."

"She won't expect us to go to church, will she?"

"Don't worry. Tomorrow's Saturday, not Sunday."

"That's a relief! I remember going to church with Mother once. I thought the preacher would never stop."

The twins found Aunt Myrtle in the kitchen removing a steaming dish from the oven. A delicious smell filled the whole room. It made Eric's mouth water. He noticed another cloth-covered dish sitting on the table. He reached over to lift the cover and take a look.

"Hands off, young man!" Aunt Myrtle said. "That's for tomorrow."

Eric's hand jerked back like a bee had stung it.

"What's so special about tomorrow?" Susan asked.

"Tomorrow is a birthday-celebration day, that's what." Aunt Myrtle's eyes sparkled.

Eric cast a glance at Susan. "Oh. We're sorry. We didn't know it was your birthday."

Aunt Myrtle laughed. "It isn't my birthday. It's the birthday of the whole world." She looked into their blank faces. "I see this calls for an explanation, doesn't it? Get that car washed, Eric, and let me buy a few groceries, and I'll explain all this." With that, she snatched up her purse and walked out the door.

Susan followed obediently. She paused a moment in the doorway and shrugged at Eric, who stood staring after them.

"It's all so simple," Susan shouted at Eric as she threw open the door to his room later that afternoon.

"Hey! You came bursting in here without even knocking!" Eric complained.

"I'm sorry. I just couldn't wait to tell you. Look! Aunt Myrtle explained it so nicely." Susan flopped down on Eric's bed and opened the same little Book Aunt Myrtle had taken from her backpack earlier that day. "Aunt Myrtle says this Book has lots of answers to questions people ask."

"You found the answer to this whole birthday business in that Book? The Bible?" Eric looked amazed.

"Sure. Here it is, right in the very first part of the Book, Genesis 2. Here, you read it," Susan said, thrusting the Bible into Eric's hands.

" 'Thus the heavens and the earth were completed, and all their hosts. And by the seventh day God completed His work which He had done; and He rested on the seventh day from all His work which He had done. Then God blessed the seventh day and sanctified it, because in it He rested from all His work which God had created and made.' "* Eric stopped reading. "So Sabbath is the celebration of Creation. Is that what she meant? But what does that word *sanctified* mean?"

"It means that the Sabbath is a day set apart as special," Susan explained.

"How do you know God expects you to pay any attention to a special day like that?" Eric asked.

"He gave us a command to do it," Susan said. "In the book of Exodus."

Eric read the verses to himself. "It says here that God wants us to remember the seventh day and rest on it like He did. I could use some time to rest and to think."

"It isn't that kind of rest, silly. It means a change in the kind of things we do. Aunt Myrtle said that God wasn't tired after creating the world; He just wanted to make a special time when the people He created could get to know Him better. Kind of like a date."

"A date with God?" Eric felt amazed.

"Aunt Myrtle says that God knows us so well He can even tell how many hairs we have on our heads. That's why He made a special time when we could get to know Him."

"Man, I can't see taking a whole day every week to sit around and read the Bible and talk to someone I can't even see," Eric groaned. "Hey, wait!" His face brightened. "Maybe that's why Aunt Myrtle spends so much

---

*Bible texts in this chapter are from the New American Standard Bible.

time climbing around on the rocks. She finds creatures that can teach her about God. I'd like that a lot more than just sitting around all day."

"That from the mouth of one who loves to hole up in his room with the door locked and think," Susan teased.

"It's almost evening. Lets see if there's anything else to be done before Sabbath," Susan said.

"But what's so special about evening?"

"Oh, I forgot. The Bible says the Sabbath begins at sundown on Friday and goes until sundown Saturday night," Susan explained. "See, it's right here in the Bible." She opened the Bible to a marker she'd put in Leviticus 23:32. " 'From evening until evening you shall keep your sabbath.' If we keep the Sabbath as a special day, it's like a sign that we choose to be the friend of the God who created us. Aunt Myrtle made it all sound very special. I have to admit I don't understand all about it yet, but I think I'd like to."

"Yeah, all this business about a Book giving so many answers and a God who wants me to be His friend. Well, I don't know . . ." Eric looked out the window at the waves that kept returning to the shore. They seemed so strong. A person could count on them to keep on, day after day, crashing and making their music. It would be good to have someone to depend on like that . . .

"While you were gone getting all these answers about the Sabbath, I found a secret," Eric said abruptly.

"What secret?" Susan said, jumping about.

"I found it in an old shoe box in the storage shed," Eric teased. "And there's an old wooden trunk there. I'll bet it's full of old stuff."

"Let's go snoop around," Susan begged.

"I'm afraid you'll have to wait a while," Eric teased. "Isn't that Aunt Myrtle calling us?"

4

A Key for Eric

Golden fingers of morning light streamed through Eric's window and danced about the room. Sounds of dishes clattering together nudged his sleepy mind. He yawned and stretched, blinking into the warm sunlight.

"Hey, Eric, are you up?" Susan's cheerful voice ran up the steps and joined the sun in Eric's room.

"Of course I'm up," he called, glancing at the clock on the night stand. "It's almost ten o'clock." He pulled on a pair of faded jeans and an old T-shirt, then rummaged through his bottom dresser drawer until he found two socks that matched.

"Are you coming down?" Susan called again.

Eric grabbed his tennis shoes, ran his fingers through his blond hair, and headed for the stairs. "Can't you wait—?" he started to say. Then a wonderful aroma floated up the stairwell and caught him like a lasso and pulled him into the kitchen. Susan stood at the stove, almost engulfed in Aunt Myrtle's frilly apron. She poured pancake batter from a dipper on a sizzling frying pan.

"Smells good," Eric complimented.

Susan turned toward him, dripping batter on her tennis shoes. "Hungry?" she asked.

Eric sat down and sampled the grapefruit that someone

had neatly cut into sections. He watched Susan turn a bubbling pancake. She smiled out of two large brown eyes that talked even when she didn't. He thought again how they were set just right above her round pink cheeks.

"Here you go." Susan plopped three ragged pancakes onto his plate, then dropped into a chair.

Eric smeared butter over the pancakes and poured syrup on top until it spilled over the plate's edge onto the table.

"Aunt Myrtle left this food for us before she went to church."

Eric said nothing. He continued to stuff pancake into his mouth.

"I wish you hadn't been so rude to her last evening when she invited us to go along."

Eric felt a pang of regret as he remembered his harsh words. "Well, you didn't want to go to church either, did you?"

"I don't know. Maybe." Susan rolled up a sleeve of her baggy shirt and reached down to roll up her pant legs.

"I just don't like a bunch of strange people staring at me," Eric grumbled. He took the last bite of pancake and washed it down with orange juice. "Looks like you're getting ready to go somewhere," he said.

"Want to go with me?" Susan reached into the pocket of her blue cotton pants and pulled out a plastic bag. "We could do some collecting. Aunt Myrtle won't be home for three hours."

"Nope," Eric said. He grabbed one of Susan's braids and gave it a jerk. She jumped up and started after him, waving the greasy spatula.

Eric evaded her easily. He liked to see her braids jump about. They were thick and shiny and curled up at the ends.

"I'm going treasure hunting in the storage shed. The old chest is out there somewhere. I saw it when I cleaned out my room, remember?"

Susan followed Eric to the storage building. The door creaked open. Darkness and musty smells jumped out at them. They searched the room in the dim light cast by a single light bulb dangling by a yellow cord from the ceiling.

"Here is is!" Eric shouted. He tugged the heavy chest into the center of the room.

"Phew, it's dusty!" Susan coughed. She crouched down beside Eric.

"Of course. It's probably been sitting here for years." Eric pulled a large bunch of keys that were tied together with string from his pocket. "I found them in the den," he said, ignoring Susan's surprised glance. "Aunt Myrtle keeps lots of keys there." One by one, he poked each key into the keyhole, twisting and jiggling it. Nothing happened. Then the last key—a long, thin one with a heavy-toothed end—slipped right in and turned easily.

"Who's that?" Susan gasped, jumping to her feet.

"Oh, no, it's Aunt Myrtle!" Eric groaned. "Quick! Help me get the chest back in its place."

The twins pushed the chest against the wall, hastily brushed themselves off, and crept to the door of the shed. Eric pulled the light cord, leaving them in darkness.

A car door slammed, and Aunt Myrtle's voice rang out, "God is my Father, Jesus is my brother, and the blessed Holy Spirit is my guide . . ."

"What's she singing about?" Eric whispered.

"I don't know," Susan answered. "Something about God, Jesus, and a spirit of some sort. I hope she goes inside right now."

Aunt Myrtle disappeared into the house, still singing the strange song.

"Whatever, we'd better get out of here," Eric muttered. "Come on!"

They found Aunt Myrtle staring at the cluttered kitchen, lips pursed together and brows drawn into a frown.

"We got busy just looking around . . . the time went so fast . . ." Susan blurted an answer to the question no one asked.

"I see." Aunt Myrtle looked at both of them until they wiggled under her stare, but said nothing more. The twins cleaned up the kitchen and sat through lunch without many words.

"We'll go for a walk and investigate some tide pools," Aunt Myrtle announced when they finished eating. "It'll be good to get outside for a while."

They climbed down the steps to the beach and walked to the tide-pool area at the foot of the cliffs.

"Take a good look at these pools," Aunt Myrtle instructed as they crouched near the edge. "They're just chock-full of life. You'll see it once you sit still for a few minutes." She scooted a little closer to the edge. "The interesting thing is that God intended each plant and animal to live together and to benefit each other. When Jesus and God and the Holy Spirit worked together to make all this beauty, They planned for everything to live in peace and to be beautiful. I wish I could have been there in the beginning to see it as They made it." She sighed.

The three sat in silence gazing into the clear pool. Eric saw a tiny orange starfish clinging to the rocks and several green flowerlike things waving tiny arms in the water. He watched small crabs bob along beneath

TREASURES BY THE SEA

pointed black shells. He thought about the life in the tide pool and the life that people shared on land.

Susan looked up. "Aunt Myrtle, I was thinking about the three Gods in your song. Are they real?"

"Certainly, Susan. There are three different Beings. We call Them a Trinity. They all have the same loving character and work toward the same goals. Paul, one of God's special friends, mentioned Their names when he said farewell to his Christian friends. He said he wanted 'the grace of the Lord Jesus Christ, and the love of God, and the fellowship of the Holy Spirit' to be with them [2 Corinthians 13:14, NIV]. The Bible is full of stories in which each of Them worked in different ways to help people."

"Could you sing the song for us again?" Susan asked.

Aunt Myrtle's voice rang out over the tide pools and drifted away into the wind. Eric couldn't get the last words out of his head. "I'm part of the family in the sky." Perhaps God did know about families and how he felt about being part of a family in which everyone loved each other. It seemed a bit unreal.

"And," Aunt Myrtle added, "there are thousands of angels living in heaven. They all live in peace and joy together."

"Is God the leader of everything, then?" Susan asked.

"You could say it that way. Jesus is equal with God, but He chose to come to our world to help us understand how much we are loved. He also came to save us from our sins. After He rose from the dead and returned to heaven, the Holy Spirit came to be with us. He has the power to be with each person who wants Him. It's a heavenly family all working together for our happiness."

"Wow," Susan sighed. She gazed into the tide pool that the family of sea creatures lived in. Even in this

30

lovely place, Susan knew tragedy existed. She wondered if there ever had been a place in which creatures or people lived in peace like the family in heaven.

"Look," Aunt Myrtle pointed. "See those seaweeds that live in the strong currents? They look exactly like miniature palm trees. Scientists call them sea palms."

Eric and Susan stretched out over the far side of the pool toward the pounding surf. The foam and water swirled around several tiny green sea palms and tried to tear them from the rocks upon which they seemed to be rooted.

"What holds them there?" Eric shouted. "Why didn't they come loose?"

"It's the holdfasts. There's a mass of tiny fibers that cling to the rocks. They always make me think of the fine threads of courage and love that pass between God and those who love Him. Waves of trouble can't tear us loose from trusting in God."

Susan looked at Eric's reflection flickering in the clear water. She could see a frown form around his mouth. He jumped up and jammed his hands in his pockets. He started off down the beach toward the house. Susan started to run after him, but Aunt Myrtle held her back.

"Let him go, Susan. He's just thinking. Don't worry. There's a key that will fit just right, and it will unlock his sad heart. You'll see."

Susan looked at Aunt Myrtle in amazement. *I hope so. I do hope so,* she thought.

5

The In-and-Out-Laws

Susan sat hunched up on the window seat. She twisted the edges of a plump pink pillow. Two tears formed tiny pools in the corners of her brown eyes, then spilled over and ran down her cheeks before she could wipe them away. She leaned her head against the windowpane, ignoring the shimmering golden California poppies that nodded from the garden below.

She felt like she needed to talk to someone about the ache inside. But who could help her with a vague loneliness she didn't fully understand herself?

Eric sat hidden away in his room, sketching. Aunt Myrtle had fled to her desk to do some writing as soon as the lunch dishes were done. With a sigh, Susan got up and wandered around the room for a few minutes. Then she crept down the stairs and peered through a door that stood slightly ajar.

Aunt Myrtle sat at a large roll-top desk, busily scribbling words onto a stack of blank paper. Susan watched her wad up a piece of paper and toss it onto the floor, where it joined other rejected papers. Sometimes she scratched the words quickly. Other times she doodled in the margins for minutes at a time. It seemed like a strange way to write, but Susan didn't dare disturb her aunt to ask questions.

Susan pushed the door open a little wider and scanned the room with curious eyes. A tall vase filled with wildflowers stood on a table near an overstuffed chair. The room was a bit cluttered, yet everything seemed to hold an important place. Seashells decorated tables and shelves and even sat in the windowsill next to crabs and sea fans.

She counted fifteen different kinds of pine cones in a basket beside the small brick fireplace in the far corner of the room. A glass case against one wall held bird nests of every size and shape. Susan leaned forward to get a better look at a tiny V-shaped nest. Suddenly she fell through the door and landed in a heap.

"Susan!" Aunt Myrtle's voice caught her. "Do come in!"

Susan picked herself up and started to back out of the room. "I'm sorry, Aunt Myrtle. I saw your door open and just peeked in."

"I see that for myself." Aunt Myrtle laughed. "Stay a minute. I need a break."

"What are you writing about?" Susan asked.

"I'm doing an article for a magazine. It explains the eight special laws that protect our health. You see, there was a time long ago when people lived happy, healthy lives and obeyed these laws."

"You mean that *everyone* was happy? No one ever got sick or died?"

"That's right, Susan."

"Humph! I studied history every year in school, and no one ever mentioned any time when people felt healthy and happy. Everyone has always been fighting and killing each other."

The unexpected voice from the doorway made Aunt Myrtle and Susan jump. They turned around to see Eric leaning against the doorjamb.

3—T.B.T.S.

"Why, Eric, hello!" Aunt Myrtle said at last.

"Eavesdropper Eric!" Susan teased.

"Nope, just passing by." Eric turned to leave.

"Join us, Eric," Aunt Myrtle said. "I was just telling Susan about the eight ways that these people stayed happy and healthy."

"What people?" Eric demanded.

"You'll find their names and story in the very first book of the Bible. They lived in a place called Eden, and I can assure you they were perfectly happy for a long time."

"But how?" Susan asked.

"You see, the very first people God created felt good all the time. They had strong bodies because they obeyed the Creator's laws for health," Aunt Myrtle explained.

"I bet one of the laws was about using plenty of pure water," Eric suggested. "Our science teacher said our bodies are about two-thirds water."

"That's right, Eric. Can you guess another law, Susan?"

"I think exercise should be a health law. When people run and jump and climb hills, they get stronger, and it makes the lungs work. The heart too," Susan said.

"And, Susan, with all that happening, the body can cleanse itself on the inside much easier. So you feel better and live longer."

"Well, if you need to move around a lot, then how about rest? Isn't that important too?" Eric asked.

"Eric just wants to know if it's OK to sit around and read all day," Susan teased.

"Susan just likes to hoppity hop through her day," Eric retorted, making a face at her.

"You're both right. Actually, too little rest or exercise isn't God's plan, but neither is too much. We need to remember to keep things in balance. Getting fresh, pure air while we exercise or sleep is another law God made for us to remember," Aunt Myrtle said.

Eric sat down in the big chair. "I know that one. That's why Dad talked me out of trying cigarettes with the guys at school. He said I wouldn't be very good at running, and I'd damage my lungs. That would mess up a lot of things."

Aunt Myrtle nodded. "Any chemicals or drugs that we take into our bodies might give us a temporary good feeling, but then we have to live with the damage they've done to us. Sometimes that's a lot to be stuck with. Don't you think that's one reason a loving God warns us about these things? He wants us to have clear minds and strong bodies so we can enjoy being alive. He has ways to help us with our problems without our poisoning ourselves to feel good for the moment."

"Is that what temperance means?" Susan asked.

"That's another of the laws—temperance. It means using the right things in the right amount for the best results to your health," Aunt Myrtle explained. "Can you guess any other laws? There are three more."

"I was thinking about sickness and germs. How do we avoid those?" Eric asked.

"One of the last laws is something you probably don't think about much because it's something you've been taught all your life. It's called cleanliness. God made water very special—it will clean almost anything. A fresh, clean house and clean clothing help us stay well."

"Wait a minute! You haven't mentioned anything about food. I'll bet there are hundreds of laws about that. Like don't eat anything that tastes good!" Eric moaned.

Aunt Myrtle laughed and reached out to yank the blond shock of hair that hung over Eric's eyes. He dodged, but not before she managed to give it one good tug.

"Eric, it all depends on how you grew up."

"Yeah, Eric's a junk-food junkie. He—"

"Susan!" Aunt Myrtle interrupted. A firm tone crept into her voice. "We all struggle with different things. Eating good food is something everyone has a problem with at least some of the time."

"What's so bad about snacks and junk food? I eat good things too," Eric defended.

"Let me show you something, Eric." Aunt Myrtle picked up a beautiful queen conch shell from her desk. "I've learned so much from this beautiful shell that it almost seems to be talking to me," she said.

"Wow! It's a beauty, all right." Eric took the large shell in his hands, turning it over and over. "Now that's a strong shell. I bet a big animal lived in that. I don't see how anything could get through that sturdy shell."

"And the color is so bright!" Susan added. She reached out and ran her fingers over the smooth, pearly opening, then felt along the bumpy outside.

"There's a mantle that surrounds many seashells," Aunt Myrtle explained. "The shape of that shell is determined by the shape of the mantle."

"What's the mantle like?" Susan asked.

"It's a flat slab of soft, fleshy tissue that has the ability to take calcium and minerals from the food the creature eats and secrete a liquid substance that turns hard when it touches water or air. So the strength and shape of the shells depend on what the animal eats and the shape of the mantle edge. This conch is shaped by a mantle that had frilled edges. That's why it isn't smooth, but has bumps."

"But what about that shell?" Susan asked, pointing to a spotted brown shell on the windowsill. She picked it up and ran her fingers over the smooth, rounded surface.

"This is a cowrie shell, Susan. The mantle of the cowrie is flat and smooth at the edges. It wraps all the way around this shell and gives it a glossy finish."

"How does a shell come to have two halves, like clams do?" Eric asked.

"That's easy, Eric. In that case the mantle has two lobes, so it makes two shells."

"The shell is like a house that the sea creature lives in, right?" Susan asked.

"That's right, Susan. I like to think I'm like a seashell. The shape of my life is determined by what I take into my body-house and what I wrap myself up in. I've found that when I'm wrapped up in God's love and when I trust Him, my life is shaped more like I want it to be."

"Like the shape of smiles and joy?" Susan gave her aunt a shy smile.

"Yes, like that. I'll tell you about that sometime. Anyway, you now know the eighth law—trusting in God and having His love in your heart."

"I figured you'd say something about God before this thing was over." Eric groaned and rolled his eyes. "I've got to get going. Oh, Aunt Myrtle," he said, pausing in the doorway. "May I borrow that queen conch? I thought I could practice sketching a bit before supper."

"Certainly, Eric. Just return it when you're finished."

"But, Aunt Myrtle," Susan questioned. "If everyone obeyed the laws for health and happiness, why is this world such a mess and—"

"That's a good question. Let's settle it over fixing supper. It has to do with good news and bad news."

The two went arm in arm into the bright kitchen. Eric could hear their laughter all the way to the top of the stairs, where he stood looking at the queen conch shell.

6

Hooked

W hat in the world am I going to fix for supper?"
Aunt Myrtle groaned.
Susan watched as she rummaged through the
cans and boxes on the pantry shelves.

"There's only one thing we can do in a case like this,"
Aunt Myrtle said, throwing up her hands in a gesture of
mock despair. "Let's eat out!"

"Can we really?" Susan squealed, jumping from her
chair and running to the door. "Eric, hurry up! We're
going to eat Mexican food at last." Susan turned toward
Aunt Myrtle. "We can, can't we? Please say yes."

"It looks like everything's been decided." Aunt Myrtle
laughed.

"Hey, wait a minute!" Eric called down the stairwell.
He arrived almost instantly in the kitchen doorway,
jeans rolled up and tennies tied together by the laces
and slung over his shoulder. One hand held a camera
and the other waved randomly at Aunt Myrtle and
Susan.

"You don't want to eat?" Susan sounded shocked.

"Of course I do," Eric said, "but look!" He took Susan
by the arm and led her to the living room window. Her
breath caught in her throat. A cloudless sky stretched as
far as the eyes could see. The sun, a golden blazing

sphere, hovered just above a great finger of cliff that jutted into the sea. The sky was a great apricot-colored curtain shimmering behind sun and cliff.

"Look at that perfect silhouette!" Susan shouted. She traced its outline against the windowpane with one finger, following the rocky outline, then up over two palm trees and down the cliff into the sea. "Wow! It's beautiful, Eric." She turned toward him. The room was empty.

Susan flung the door open and ran down the steps to the beach. She soon found Aunt Myrtle and Eric bending over their cameras, discussing the best angle for taking pictures. She heard the click, click of shutters and watched Eric sprawl in the sand, waiting for the moment the sun would drop behind the cliff. She almost expected to hear a splash when it did.

Several sea gulls waddled along the wet sand, casting little black shadows onto the beach. Susan laughed and walked toward them. Instantly they flew up, squawking and scolding her. As she walked back up the beach toward Aunt Myrtle and Eric, she saw a fat, fluffy gull hunched up on the sand.

Susan slid her feet slowly over the sand, moving toward the old gull. His eye popped open, and a folded wing twitched. He made several jerky movements, then flopped onto the sand.

That's strange, Susan thought. *Gulls squawk and waddle and soar. They even rest on the sand sometimes. But they don't act like that!* She stooped down to take a closer look. The gull tried to stand up. Wings and legs seemed all tangled together. He struggled to open his mouth and scream at her, but no sound came out. His neck seemed tied to his back.

"Aunt Myrtle, come quick! Something's wrong with

this gull." She ran sobbing to Aunt Myrtle.

"Be still, Susan!" Aunt Myrtle commanded. They moved a little closer to the sea gull in the sand. "Don't go any nearer. We are just frightening him." Aunt Myrtle studied the gull in the dim light.

"Look!" Eric pointed to a tangle of fishing line near the gull. "I think he has swallowed a fishhook. The line is wound all around him. That's why he can't get up, even though he is afraid of us."

"I believe you're right, Eric." Aunt Myrtle turned suddenly. "Susan, we're going to make a phone call. Eric, you stay here and look after things."

Eric sat down in the sand far enough from the gull so that it didn't struggle anymore. Aunt Myrtle and Susan disappeared into the gathering darkness. Soon he saw the beams of two flashlights and heard voices. A tall, slender man walked beside Aunt Myrtle and Susan.

"I'm sure Eric is right." The man's voice filled the silent air. "Those gulls will eat anything. He probably mistook a fancy fisherman's fly for a tasty morsel and swallowed it in one thoughtless gulp."

"Eric, this is Dr. Foster, a friend of mine. I think he can help us," Aunt Myrtle said as they arrived at the spot where Eric sat in the sand.

"Hello, Eric." The man gave him a quick grin. "So you have a gull in trouble."

Dr. Foster looked at Susan, whose eyes seemed twice their normal size as she clung to Aunt Myrtle and stared at the stricken gull. "Perhaps the ladies would like to wait for us at the house," he said, giving Aunt Myrtle a knowing look.

"Now, Eric, let's see about this gull of yours."

The next few moments blurred together in Eric's mind. When at last they released the gull and returned to the house, he tried to pull his thoughts together. Eric couldn't erase the picture of the terror in the gull's eyes as they tried to capture it. He remembered Dr. Foster's strong yet gentle hands as he worked the horrid hook from the feeble, struggling gull. He saw again the kindness that filled Dr. Foster's eyes as he freed the gull.

"I think he has a fair chance of making it," Dr. Foster's voice continued as he told Aunt Myrtle and Susan the details. "We found him in time. Now that he's free, he'll be able to find something to eat."

"Thanks for coming, Merle." Aunt Myrtle smiled. "We all appreciate it."

Susan touched her aunt's arm. "Aunt Myrtle, remember when you were telling us about a time when everyone had health and happiness? What happened to get things into a dreadful mess like this, anyway?"

"She asks big questions!" Dr. Foster set his glass of lemonade on the table and moved closer to where Susan sat on the sofa. "Susan," he said, "that gull suffered, but I can tell you that long ago two people suffered a lot more because they thoughtlessly became hooked on an idea suggested by an old serpent."

"Hooked on what idea?" Eric asked. He sat beside Dr. Foster. "How do you know that, anyway?"

Dr. Foster picked up a book from the table. "Eric, it's right here in the first part of the Bible—the whole sad story. I call it the bad-news story. You will find this story in chapter 3 of Genesis. After you read it, we can talk about it, if you like."

The twins read the verses silently. A frown crossed Eric's face.

After a few minutes, Dr. Foster said, "It's really a sad story."

Eric looked up. "I don't believe it! After God gave

Adam and Eve everything for their happiness, they still didn't trust Him. They listened instead to the voice of a strange serpent."

"It does seem incredible, doesn't it?" said Aunt Myrtle.

"God asked them not to eat of the tree of the knowledge of good and evil?" Susan asked. "You know, it seems like they could have obeyed just that one request."

"That's right, Susan," Dr. Foster said. "God wanted them to love and obey Him out of trust that He had given them the best way to live. However, He allowed them the choice to disobey Him."

Eric shook his head. "He even warned them that the temptation would come. I mean, that they would be tested to see if they would be loyal."

"The whole thing about a talking serpent and the idea that they would become wise like God was a trick," Dr. Foster explained. "Once they swallowed the idea that God was trying to keep something good from them they disobeyed, and sin came flooding in. With it came suffering and death. I see it in my office every day. I hate the sadness that people suffer as a result of their thoughtless choices." Dr. Foster walked to the window and looked out into the night. "There's a lot of darkness in people's hearts."

Susan traced her finger over the verses that told the sad story of the once-happy pair who chose to listen to the voice of a serpent rather than obey the simple request of their Friend, God. "Oh, why did they listen to that serpent?" she cried, looking up at Dr. Foster.

"I don't really know, Susan. Perhaps it was partly because they trusted their own strength to obey God and resist the words of a stranger. They intended to obey God, I'm sure."

"That isn't all the bad news," Aunt Myrtle added.

42

"Since that time we've all been born with the tendency to do the same rebellious thing. We listen to the serpent's lies, and we mistrust God. Without a miracle, we would stay that way and die. We would never want to become God's friends. We wouldn't even want to live like He intended for us to live."

"It sounds hopeless," Eric groaned.

"About as hopeless as that gull's ever getting free of the fishhook and line. The more he struggled, the more entangled he became," Dr. Foster said.

"Well, who is this serpent, and how can you talk about a God of love when we are caught in such a tangled mess?" Eric asked. His brows wrinkled together, and he jammed his hands into his pockets.

"Young man, there is good news. Join our class next Sabbath, and you'll find the answers. The bad-news serpent and the good-news God—that's our subject. Will I see you then?" Dr. Foster's eyes twinkled invitingly.

"What does a guy have to do around here to get answers?" Eric grumbled. "OK, I'll come this time, at least. I hope you have a pretty good answer, because I want to know how a serpent could talk. And I do want to know what the good news is."

"Good!" Dr. Foster thrust out a large hand to Eric. "And thank you, young man, for helping me free a sea gull from his misery. You've got the makings of a good veterinarian, I'd say." He walked to the door. "Myrtle, I must go. I have surgery in the morning." He flashed the twins a grin. "See you two in a couple of days, then."

Eric thought about the tall, friendly man as he waved goodbye. He really did enjoy helping with the gull. It was even better than playing catcher for the home team. Just maybe he had made a new friend.

7

Villains and Heroes

Y ou will remember that last week we studied
about the bad-news serpent—"

Eric recognized Dr. Foster's voice. He and
Susan stood and stared at the door, then turned a questioning look at Aunt Myrtle. She motioned for them to go inside. "A person could get lost around here, so I'll meet you right here at 10:45. Have a good time, and let me know if you find out who that serpent is." Aunt Myrtle laughed and walked briskly away.

Eric nudged Susan into the room ahead of him. They slipped into two empty seats in the back row.

"Whew, we timed that just right," Eric whispered into Susan's ear. "I just hate coming into a roomful of strange people. See, they're all so busy they didn't even notice us."

"Well, I don't like it," Susan complained. "How can I meet any friends this way? Hey, that's got to be Margo, the girl I met at the store last Friday when Aunt Myrtle and I went shopping." Susan pointed toward the front row where five girls sat. They held black books open on their laps.

"The one with the long blond hair?" Eric whispered.

"Yes. I'll introduce you to her after class if you like."

"Don't be dumb," Eric grumbled. "I intend to meet

some of these guys and find out if any of them knows what a baseball looks like. Then maybe—"

"Shh, I want to hear what he's saying." Susan gave Eric a friendly poke in the ribs.

"Now let's review what we learned about that villainous serpent for the benefit of those who missed last week's lesson," Dr. Foster said, smiling at Eric and Susan. "Can anyone tell me what happened to Lucifer, 'son of the morning'?"

"I can," said a voice belonging to the golden-haired girl in the front row.

"All right, Margo," Dr. Foster encouraged.

Susan noticed that Eric suddenly sat up straight and leaned forward. She smiled to herself.

"He was cast out of heaven because he wanted to take Jesus' place and become like God. I think he was jealous."

"Good, Margo. Did he always feel like that?"

"I don't think so."

"Can you give me a text to support your answer?" Dr. Foster persisted. "The rest of you check Margo's answer to see if she's correct."

The sound of pages being flipped filled the silent room. Eric and Susan looked at one another in surprise.

"The answer is in Ezekiel 28:14, 15," Margo called out.

Dr. Foster read the verses in his strong, clear voice. "Anyone else have an idea?" he asked.

"Isaiah 14:13 and 14 tell us that Satan wanted to be greater than God," a boy with red hair and freckles put in. "How could he expect to do that?"

"He couldn't, of course. God created him, so Satan could never become greater than the Creator. What did his rebellious behavior cause?" Dr. Foster asked the class.

"War!" a boy with blond hair and freckles shouted.

Everyone laughed, including Dr. Foster.

"You bet, John," Dr. Foster said. "Now show me a text to support that."

"That's easy," John said. He fumbled with his Bible for a moment. "It says so in Revelation 12:7."

"You have it correct, John." Dr. Foster smiled. "Can anyone tell me what names the Bible gives to Lucifer?"

"Sure," a voice called out. A tall, thin boy stood to his feet. He gave Dr. Foster a grin. Eric thought he saw a flash of mischief in the boy's blue eyes.

"The other names are Satan, the dragon, the devil, and—"

"And the serpent!" a girl's voice broke in. She blushed red when she realized she had spoken out of turn.

"Great!" Dr. Foster said. "And as you remember, this Satan used the form of a serpent when he tempted Eve to sin. He is the bad-news villain. He is right down here on the earth tempting people to distrust God. His business is to destroy. In fact, he brought death to our world."

Susan's hand shot up. "What's it like to be dead? I mean, what happens to people when they die? Where are they?" she asked.

Everyone turned to stare at her. Eric wanted to dissolve into thin air. He managed a weak smile, but he could feel his face burning. It felt like it might burst into flames.

"That's an important question, Susan. Can you answer it, class?"

After what seemed like an eternity, the curious faces turned away one by one, and each person began to search through the Bibles that lay on their laps. The sounds of rustling pages once again filled the silent room.

The next half hour passed rapidly as the class attempted to give answers to Susan's question. Eric forgot to be embarrassed as the discussion continued. He felt relieved when Kevin moved to the back row to share a Bible with him.

They felt quite reluctant to leave when Aunt Myrtle found them at the door and ushered them into the church. Eric and Susan hardly heard a word Pastor Brown spoke. Their heads fairly danced with thoughts put there by the verses the students had shared with them. At long last the sermon ended, and they endured the last introduction.

"And those kids actually found the answers to Dr. Foster's questions in their Bibles!" Eric burst out once they had started off in Aunt Myrtle's red Cougar.

"The serpent, he's the devil!" Susan interjected. "He caused death to come into our world."

"Did you know the Bible says that dead people don't know anything? That they just sleep until Jesus comes again?" Eric asked.

"That's right, Eric," Aunt Myrtle said. "What did you think happened at death?"

"I guess I didn't think much about it until—" His voice trailed off uncertainly.

"Until Mother died," Susan finished.

"Maybe I thought God was cruel because He sent people to hell to burn for years and years unless they had done enough good things to get into heaven," Eric said. "I'm glad we don't worship a God like that. He is loving and wise. He wants us to understand these things." Aunt Myrtle smiled at the two serious faces beside her.

"Dr. Foster explained that Lucifer became a villain, but that God is a hero. He said there's a lot of good news to talk about next week."

"There are a lot of strange new ideas for me to think about," Eric said. "I just don't know."

"Eric, life is like that. Learning new ideas can be confusing. But I hope you'll check these things out for yourself," Aunt Myrtle encouraged.

"One thing that I don't understand is if the soul doesn't go to heaven or to a place of punishment, where does it go?" Susan asked.

"Here, let me show you something." Eric pulled a folded piece of paper from his pocket. "Kevin showed me an equation from a Bible verse. I think it's from Genesis 2:7."

Susan looked at Eric in surprise, but she didn't say the thought that flashed through her mind. It felt good to have Eric explaining something to her again. She looked at the words on the wrinkled paper: Body + Breath = Living Soul.

"If you remove the breath from the body, there is no living soul," Eric explained. "The soul is a result of a combination of breath from God and a body. So when a person dies, his body returns to the earth and his breath returns to God."

"Good, Eric!" Aunt Myrtle praised. "That's a very good way to explain the subject. By the way, did you talk about the good news?"

"We never got to that," Eric complained. "Susan blurted out her question about being dead."

"Perhaps you didn't have the courage to ask what you wondered about yourself," Aunt Myrtle suggested, giving Eric a meaningful look.

"Would you like to invite some friends for a walk today?" Aunt Myrtle asked, steering the conversation in another direction.

"Oh, yes!" Susan clapped her hands together. "I want to invite Margo and Dr. Foster." She gave Eric a quick wink.

"Invite whomever you please." Eric made a face at Susan. "Anyway, I would like to ask Kevin."

Susan noticed that Aunt Myrtle's face wore a small frown. "Did you already ask Dr. Foster?" Aunt Myrtle asked. She brought the car to a stop near the front door.

"Not exactly. But he's going to be alone today and—"

"Maybe you ought to let Aunt Myrtle invite her own friends." Eric gave Susan an impatient look.

"I only thought that—" Susan started.

"It's all right, Susan. However, Eric does have a point. Now get changed, and I'll make some phone calls."

"Women," Eric grumbled. "Always playing cupid." He searched under a pile of clothes for a missing sneaker.

"Sometimes Auntie looks lonely," Susan defended. She flopped onto Eric's bed and jammed her feet into her sneakers. "A big empty house like this doesn't make much sense."

Eric lunged under the bed and came out with a dusty shoe. "By the look on her face, you better knock off the meddling," Eric bossed.

"You mean you aren't curious about her or that old chest anymore?" Susan teased.

"Certainly I am!" Eric threw his shoulders back and thrust a fist into the air. "Very soon I intend to continue the quest for knowledge like a true explorer. But right now all I want to do is explore the strawberry pie on the pantry shelf. Let's go!"

8

A Hero With Good News

Honk! Honk! The shrill blast of Dr. Foster's horn startled Susan. She dropped the last of the clean spoons into the drawer and pushed it shut.

"They're here!" Susan shouted.

Eric appeared with a sketch pad under one arm and a bulging pack slung over his shoulder.

Margo and Kevin waved from the Jeep.

"Let's get things stowed away and be off," Dr. Foster called cheerily when Aunt Myrtle, Eric, and Susan arrived in the driveway moments later.

"What a perfect day!" Aunt Myrtle sighed as they sped away.

"I think we should head for a beach north of Santa Barbara," Dr. Foster suggested. "I believe we'd have a better chance of discovering shorebirds and shells."

"That sounds fine to me, Merle," Aunt Myrtle agreed.

They rode along enjoying the warm sunshine, laughter, and chatter filling every corner of the Jeep. Gradually, the cluttered beach towns gave way to open country, where rolling hills wore wildflowers amid their wigs of waving grasses.

"Aunt Myrtle, would you tell us a story?" Margo asked, leaning forward.

"Tell the twins about Hezekiah's tunnel," Kevin suggested.

"Oh, yes!" Susan cried. She bounced up and down on the back seat. A flying braid swished across Eric's face.

"Duck, everyone! A low-flying helicopter is among us," Eric teased. He exchanged a mischievous look with Kevin. The boys fell to the floor in mock terror.

"Perhaps we might have a safer trip to the sea if we tie them all up back there." Dr. Foster gave Aunt Myrtle a quick grin. Susan thought his eyes sparkled like the noonday sun on the blue waves.

"OK, kids," Aunt Myrtle began. "Last spring when I visited Jerusalem, I decided to go through Hezekiah's tunnel. I joined a group who thought themselves brave enough to make the journey. We rolled up our pants and buttoned our sweaters. At the bottom of the stone steps leading to the entrance of the low, narrow tunnel, a man handed our group leader a flickering candle. He counted off five people, then sent them into the darkness. Our group entered one by one behind our leader. A moist smell filled our nostrils, and the chill of frigid water clutched at our ankles. Suddenly a draft from the entrance snuffed out our light."

"What a horrid place to be," Susan blurted.

"Yes, Susan. The darkness seemed to wrap itself around us like a thick blanket. No one moved. Finally someone in the group managed to locate a match, and the candle glowed once more. Just a small light, but it seemed wonderful. We trudged ahead, going deeper and deeper into the long passage. I felt the walls pressing in around me. A slick layer of moisture covered the cold rock walls. We could hear the voices of others ahead but couldn't see them.

"All at once my right foot sank into a deep hole, and the frigid water reached up to my knee. I screamed, and my voice echoed off the rock walls. After that, we decided to have our leader call out when he discovered a rough spot, or a low overhanging rock might prove dangerous. We inched our way along, holding onto the shirttail of the person ahead and singing. The leader beamed his light ahead, then turned to signal that we could advance. At times the darkness seemed to reach out to squeeze us like something real and terrible. After forty-five minutes of stumbling along, we caught a glimpse of light ahead. The opening at last! Soon, strong arms reached down and drew us into the light of day. Everyone cheered and sang out with joy. Each group wanted to know how the others had gotten along."

"I remember that you said one group made the entire journey with no light at all. Many had cuts and bruises from sharp rocks," Kevin said.

"Remember the group that took a strong flashlight with them? When their candle flickered out, they had plenty of light," Margo added.

"Boy, I would have stuck with the group that had a strong light," Eric said.

"Jesus is like the strong light, Eric. The closer we stay to Him during our journey through life, the more light He can give us," Dr. Foster said thoughtfully.

No one spoke for a minute, thinking about Aunt Myrtle's story. Finally Susan spoke.

"I bet it was a dark day when Adam and Eve sinned," she said. "They must have thought nothing would ever be good again."

Margo nodded. "I think you're right. I'm glad that Jesus came to this world to die for us. Without that, we'd be lost in a darkness like that tunnel. Like John 3:16 says, God loved us so much that He gave His Son, so that whoever believes in Him won't have to die."

"But why did Jesus have to come here, and why did

He die for us?" Eric asked. "Couldn't He just kill evil Satan or something?"

"First of all, Eric, the end result of sin is death. Jesus died to pay the penalty of sin. He took our place. He actually did more than die for us. He lived for us."

"Lived for us? I don't get it," Eric protested.

"Just as the candle gave us light to see our way through the tunnel deep beneath Jerusalem's walls, Jesus lived here with us so that we could know what kind of life we should strive to live. He lives as an example for us."

"That's why God gave us the Bible too," Susan said. "Margo just showed me in her Bible where a king named David said the Bible is like a lamp."

"That's great, Margo!" Dr. Foster praised. "Myrtle, I get so excited when these knobby heads remember the verses we've studied in class." He started to whistle a snappy tune.

"But you didn't say why God couldn't just destroy Satan or something," Eric prompted.

"Hey, He couldn't do that! Everyone would go around scared. 'You disobeyed. *Zap! You're gone!*' " Kevin pointed a finger at an imaginary sinner.

"Be real!" Susan exclaimed. "God wouldn't do that."

"I guess He really did have a problem," Eric admitted.

Aunt Myrtle continued. "He loved us so much that He decided to live among us and actually become one of us. He lived a life of loving service to others and then allowed angry men to kill Him on a cross. When He arose from the dead, He returned to heaven. He sent the Holy Spirit to be with us and to give us power to obey Him and live for Him. That was His solution to the problem," Aunt Myrtle finished.

Troubled thoughts tumbled around inside Eric's mind.

53

Why hadn't anyone explained these things to him before? It all seemed so complicated. He glanced at Susan. She wore an expression of peace. *She trusts what Aunt Myrtle tells her,* he thought to himself. *Not me! I am going to find a Bible in the storage shed and read for myself. I don't know if I want Jesus to be my friend.*

The Jeep slowed down and turned onto a dirt road leading to the beach. Doors flew open, and everyone scrambled out.

"Come on, Eric!" Kevin called. "Let's go for a walk and collect driftwood."

The boys pulled off their shoes and socks and ran across the warm sand to the water's edge. Driftwood lay scattered along the beach. They chose the best pieces, filling their packs with the twisted wood. After an hour they returned to where the others sat in the sand. Aunt Myrtle and Dr. Foster studied the pages of a worn-out bird guide and gazed at the fleeting forms of birds as they sailed away over the sea. The girls formed shapes of flowers and people with the wet sand.

Eric pulled some driftwood from his pack. "Look at this wood. It looks kind of neat. I don't know what use it would be to anyone, though." He took out his knife and tried to carve one small round piece.

"Not good for much except burning," said Dr. Foster.

"How does a tree get turned into a soft, useless thing like that?" Susan asked. She turned a twisted piece over in her hands. "Trees are hard. This wood is so soft."

"It just tumbles over the sand in the wind, Susan, and the waves wash it over and over. The sun bleaches it out year after year," Aunt Myrtle said.

Eric selected a piece of driftwood. He jammed it into the sand and settled himself nearby. Soon a neat sketch of the wood began to form on the paper he held on his knees. Eric sighed with pleasure. *Dad would like this picture.* He drew a gull and added the faint shape of crashing waves. As he drew he wondered. Would his life be like a piece of wood tossed about by waves and baked in the sun? Was God real? Did God really love people enough to come and die for them?

All too soon the sun moved toward the horizon and plunged into the sea. Aunt Myrtle finished taking several photographs; then they packed up their things and started home. Within minutes everyone in the back seat had fallen asleep.

"We're home, Eric, Susan." Aunt Myrtle's voice broke into the dream that moved across the screen of Eric's mind. He awoke with a jerk. Susan popped awake beside him. The others stirred restlessly.

"See you later," Dr. Foster's voice announced.

Susan and Eric gathered up their gear and stumbled into the house and up to their rooms.

"Don't you want to see your mail?" Aunt Myrtle called after them. "There's a letter from your father."

Suddenly Eric was wide awake. He ran down the stairs and almost fell over Susan in his rush to get to the kitchen, where Aunt Myrtle stood, waving an envelope.

The twins grabbed the envelope and headed for Eric's room. They spread out the white sheets of paper on the bed and read the words that shouted at them.

I'm coming for a visit. . . . It's too lonely here without you . . . next week . . .

Eric and Susan grabbed each other and danced around the room. Next week! They would see Father. Susan scampered off to tell Aunt Myrtle the good news, and Eric tucked the letter inside a book on his desk. *How long could a whole week be?* he wondered.

9

Eric's Brittle Star

Eric groaned. He pulled the covers over his head and curled into a tight ball, trying to shut out the drone of a vacuum cleaner. He reached out and yanked the pillows over his head.

"What's all the noise around here?" he grumbled out loud.

Then instantly he threw back the blankets and jumped out of bed. Jamming his legs into a pair of blue jeans that hung over a chair back, he grabbed his blue plaid shirt from a pile of clothes on the floor.

"Hey, wait for me!" he yelled down the stairs. He sat on the top stair and tugged at his tangled shoelaces.

"Sleepyhead!" Susan teased, poking her head around the corner, laughing at the sight of Eric in his rumpled clothes.

Eric ran his fingers through the blond hair that hung over his forehead and nearly tumbled down the stairs in his hurry. "I'll vacuum. Why don't you go dust or something?" he said. "Don't you think I want to help get things ready for Dad's visit?"

"Be careful!" Susan screamed as he backed into a table. Aunt Myrtle's crystal lamp teetered back and forth, and Susan grabbed it just before it fell to the floor. Suddenly Aunt Myrtle stood in the doorway. Her eyes scanned the room, and she sighed.

"I have an idea," she said finally. "Why don't we start this day over again? How about a good breakfast and a short walk before we get into the work around here? I think we can spare a few moments since we have three days before your father arrives."

As soon as they ate breakfast and stowed the dirty dishes in the dishwasher, everyone headed down the steps and onto the sand. Aunt Myrtle climbed up over the bare rocks and settled herself on a flat place where she could watch the waves dash against the cliff's pointed toes. Eric and Susan perched nearby.

"I always like to have worship before I start my day," Aunt Myrtle explained. "Things always seem to go better that way. If you like, you may join me."

Susan didn't move, so Eric stayed where he was. He listened to Aunt Myrtle's voice as she read some verses from her Operator's Manual. Many of the words didn't make much sense to him, but Aunt Myrtle always seemed to be able to explain them. After a few minutes Aunt Myrtle said a short prayer. Eric was curious about what people said to God, so he listened carefully.

". . . and help us to have faith in You as our Father and Saviour from sin. Amen," she finished.

Eric gazed into the tide pool below his feet. He saw the image of a boy reflected in the water. He wore a rumpled shirt and jeans, but what Eric noticed most was the frown on the boy's face and the troubled eyes. *That boy is me,* he groaned to himself.

Suddenly he noticed a small creature about the size of a penny with five thin, prickly arms that twitched in every direction. He grabbed for the creature as it scrambled beneath a rock.

"Careful! That's a brittle star, and it will drop those

arms if you touch it roughly," Aunt Myrtle said. Eric saw her face reflected in the pool beside his. Her eyes sparkled in a friendly smile.

Aunt Myrtle lifted the rock and gently picked the brittle star up with her fingers.

"What do you have?" Susan asked, inching her way around the other side of the tide pool. She slipped on a piece of seaweed and landed with a splash in the cool water. Aunt Myrtle dropped the brittle star, and it escaped beneath the rough rocks.

Susan scraped the long green seaweed from her arm. "I'm sorry. Did it get away?"

"I'm afraid so," Aunt Myrtle said. "You startled me a bit too, Susan."

"How dumb!" Eric mumbled. He saw his pouty face reflected in the clear pool.

"I'm afraid Eric is a bit like that brittle star," Aunt Myrtle commented. "I've had a hard time collecting good specimens because they're quite touchy, shall we say."

The three sat in silence for some time, staring into the pool. The brittle star moved from the rocky place to seek a better hiding spot. Eric noticed that two of the arms had fallen off. It looked so ugly now.

"Let's go back now," Susan said. "It isn't much fun around here when people are so grouchy." She gave Eric a poke, turned up her nose, and climbed down the rocks toward the sandy beach.

"I'm sorry to spoil things." Eric looked at Aunt Myrtle.

"I understand more than you think, Eric. You'd laugh if you could see how grumpy I was once. That seems a long time ago now. People tend to feel that way when things go wrong with life and they can't sort things out. It takes time, Eric."

"You, a grump?" Eric looked at her in disbelief. "You

always seem pretty happy to me. Your eyes shine a lot. Mother always said people's eyes shine when they're happy. I noticed that in the reflection in the tide pool." Eric felt suddenly shy. He hadn't meant to say so much.

Aunt Myrtle placed her hand on the boy's shoulder. "Eric, when I was just twelve everything in my life turned inside out. I had my heart broken, and I felt angry, hurt, and confused. Maybe you feel that way right now. Life just doesn't work out as we plan for it to sometimes. Without knowing Jesus as a friend, I would have become a bitter old lady." She smiled at him.

"How did you become a Christian, Aunt Myrtle? I just can't seem to believe all that. Mother tried to share some things with me when she went to some meetings. It didn't make any sense. But now—"

"That's it, Eric! We are such funny creatures. It isn't until we realize that we can't handle life alone that we begin to cast about for some help. Some people try drugs, alcohol, buying new things, running around—anything to keep so busy they can't think about their problems. Some even try suicide."

"And you tried God?"

"Actually, He tried me, Eric. I'd already become a Christian, but I didn't really know Jesus as a friend. Nor did I trust Him."

"What did you do?"

"I decided to find out if I could love Him and trust Him with my life. So I read a lot about Him and tried talking to Him. I figured that if He kept His promises to others, He would keep them to me. Then something happened. It's still happening."

"A miracle? *Zap!* and you became different?"

"No," Aunt Myrtle laughed. "A process started. Everyone is born with a small amount of faith."

"I don't understand what faith is. I don't think I have any. Susan does, but I don't." Eric kicked a piece of driftwood with his wet sneaker.

"Eric, it's one of God's promises. You do have a measure of faith. Faith is the ability to take God at His word and trust Him. It grows like a plant does when it receives food and water."

"What kind of food and water does faith need to grow?"

"Put out your arm," Aunt Myrtle commanded. "Now flex it hard."

Eric rolled up his sleeve and tightened his muscles. He smiled at the hard mound that formed on his upper arm.

"Well! That's a pretty good muscle you have there, Eric," Aunt Myrtle praised. She pressed it with her fingers. "How did you get that?"

"I used it a lot. I think it really got strong when we packed and I had to lift a lot of boxes for Father. Then of course I work out in my room every day," Eric admitted.

"Well, how did you get started?"

"I guess I was born with a small muscle, and then—I see your point." Eric grinned. "Faith doesn't grow unless we use what we have."

"That's right. And one more thing. Besides exercise, you must feed faith."

"How do you do that?" Eric asked. He felt that he was beginning to believe his aunt. It seemed to work for her.

"Now, Eric"—Aunt Myrtle stopped and faced him—"prepare yourself for the easiest thing that you can imagine. God has made it very easy. The answer is in Romans 10:17. You look that up in the Bible when you get to the house. Tell me if you can see the answer."

"Come on, Aunt Myrtle, just tell me yourself."

"No, Eric. It's really important that you find the answer for yourself."

"OK, I'm going now. Susan will lend me her Bible. See you at the house." Eric ran down the wet sand, leaving footprints behind. He hurried into the house and called out, "Can I use your Bible, Susan?"

Susan appeared in the doorway. "What's going on?"

"I have to find out how to grow faith," Eric yelled. He took the stairs two at a time to Susan's desk.

"Sure, but—"

"Romans 10:17. The answer's right there. Let me look it up." Eric snatched up the Bible and started to flip through the pages. "Wow, there are a lot of pages. Where's the book of Romans, anyway?"

"Just look in the front. There's a table of contents and page numbers," Susan instructed.

"Here it is! I'll just bet the answer to growing faith isn't as easy as Aunt Myrtle says."

"Read it, Eric," Susan demanded.

" 'So then faith cometh by hearing, and hearing by the word of God' " (KJV). Eric looked at Susan, then back at the words. He sat down on the bed. "It really *is* easy. All I have to do is exercise the faith I'm born with and then read and study God's Word."

A new idea began to form in Eric's mind. Could he have faith? Really strong faith? He walked to his room and shut the door. The thought seemed so new and fragile that he wanted to let it grow a bit stronger. If he shared it right now, part of it might break away like the brittle star's arms. He couldn't risk that. Eric flipped over several pages in the Bible. His eyes rested on Ephesians 1. He read the words over and over. It seemed like the small plant of faith started to grow that very moment. Maybe he could learn to know God. Maybe!

10

The Decision

I'm sure glad Aunt Myrtle let you come today," Kevin said. He looked over the shimmering water. "This is a perfect day to jump waves."

Eric gazed at the sea spread out like a great blue blanket whose frayed edges whipped about in a blustery wind. He was supposed to swim in that madness?

"You're going to love this!" Kevin shouted over the thundering noise of the waves. "There are two parts to this stuff—getting out and getting in. Just follow me."

"I'm with you," Eric said. He swallowed the big lump in his throat.

"Now!" Kevin screamed. "Run for it!"

The two boys dashed into the frothy edge of a wave that had already tumbled onto the wet sand and had lost most of its rage. Eric felt the churning water snatch at his body. He tasted salt.

"Keep going! We have to make it out there before the next wave has a chance to build up and fall on us," Kevin shouted, still moving out fast.

Eric managed to stay right behind Kevin until suddenly he noticed a great wall of water building up in front of him. He stared at it with shocked eyes. His breath caught in his throat. Kevin just kept going out, but Eric couldn't move an inch. His eyes followed the wall of water up, up to the top of its quivering edge.

"We're too slow," Kevin shouted. "Dive into it!"

"Dive?" Eric screamed. "Are you crazy?" He turned toward the shore.

"Don't! You'll never make it," Kevin shouted. "Dive into it!"

Eric hesitated another moment. The last thing that seemed sensible was to dive into certain death.

"Like this!" Kevin shouted and disappeared into the great wall of water.

Eric tensed and plunged himself into the raging mass. To his amazement, he instantly felt himself surrounded by a calm coolness. Then *pop*, he came to the surface.

"You did it!" Kevin yelled. "Great going!"

Eric stared at the mound of water rolling toward the beach. It fell over itself onto the sand with a great crash.

"It's calm underneath. I thought I was a goner," he sputtered.

"Yeah, that churning stuff is just on the top. Get caught in it, and you'll be bounced to shore. But dive through, and it's calm underneath."

"I'm sorry I held you up. I guess I didn't believe you," Eric apologized.

Kevin laughed. "You should have seen my first try. I got a real pounding." He faced the ocean. "Now for the fun part. We stay out just far enough to avoid the falling waves and ride the swells."

The sea rose up beneath Eric, and he rode over the swell like a cork. He watched it build up and head for the shore. After riding over the mounds of water for a long time, Eric began to feel hungry and cold.

"We'll ride this one in," Kevin called across a swell.

This time Eric ignored the fear that rose up inside him. He trusted Kevin's directions completely and soon found himself moving shoreward atop a wave. It was like riding a bucking bronco that finally tossed them onto the shore. They threw themselves onto the dry sand to rest.

"That's crazy!" Eric said. "I could get used to that!"

"I knew you'd like it." Kevin grinned. "There are a lot of neat things to do around here besides baseball."

"You're right," Eric agreed. "I do miss the team a lot, though," he admitted.

"I was only kidding. I bet you're pretty good at baseball. And by the way, that was great swimming— once you got started." Kevin reached over and thumped Eric on the shoulder.

Eric wasn't used to kids handing out compliments. Maybe being a Christian did make a difference.

"I like teamwork myself," Kevin said. "Maybe that's one reason I became a Christian."

"I don't get it. How does being a Christian make you a team member?" Eric asked.

"My dad explained it like this. He said that each church member is really something like a part of the human body. You know, arms and legs and all that. Everyone is important, but different."

"I see," Eric said. He dug his hands into the wet sand and piled it up into a dripping heap.

"I think God tries to help us find Him as the answer to our problems. And if we repent, we are accepted as a member of His family."

"Repent? What do you mean?" Eric asked.

"Oh, that just means that we realize we're sinful and not loving, like God. We're sorry for the pain our sins cause God and want to change."

"I've thought about being a Christian." Eric shot a quick look at Kevin. When Kevin didn't laugh, he added, "I guess I don't feel as a Christian should."

"Dr. Foster says that feelings aren't so important in this matter. Becoming a Christian is a matter of choosing to follow Christ and accepting His death for our sins," Kevin explained. "Hey, watch out!" he shouted as a wave moved up the sand and snatched away the wall that Eric was building. The sand castle that the boys had been building melted away and disappeared with the water as it returned to the sea.

"Will you look at that!" Kevin said.

"Waves of trouble will wash away the sifting sand, but things that cling to the immovable rock are safe!" Eric intoned. "Now that's what Aunt Myrtle would say!"

"You're right about that," Kevin said. "She sees a lesson in everything."

"Say, Eric, if you're serious about being a Christian, it's easy. All you have to do is admit to God that you are a sinner and that you want a new way to live. Accept His death for your sins and ask Him to forgive you. Dr. Foster is starting a class for kids who want to be baptized and become a part of God's family. You might talk to him about it."

"Thanks, Kevin. I'll do that." Eric suddenly felt like being alone to think about things. "Let's go. I have to get ready to go with Aunt Myrtle to pick up Father at the airport." He looked at his friend shyly. "I had a great time, Kevin."

The boys headed up the beach toward Aunt Myrtle's.

"I'll call you later," Kevin called. He turned down the path, whistling.

"See you!" Eric called after him. He hurried to his room and shut the door. He knelt by his bed and started to talk to God. It wasn't easy to say what he felt, but he tried to remember what Kevin had suggested.

"Hey, Eric!" Susan burst into his room. She skidded to

a stop. "Oops, I'm sorry. What are you doing, anyway?"

"I—I'm trying to become a Christian. And I'm talking to God," Eric said, swallowing the urge to yell at Susan for forgetting to knock. "You might as well come in the rest of the way," he added.

"Do you really want to become a Christian?" Susan asked, trying to hide her surprise.

"Why else would I be down here like this, huh?"

"Eric, I do too. Can you help me?"

"Sure, it's easy. All you have to do is ask God. Of course, you have to know for sure that you don't like the way you've lived before and you must realize how awful sin is. You know, that it caused all the trouble in this world and hurts God. Stuff like that."

"I do, Eric. I know why Mother died. That man drank and didn't even know what he was doing. If he'd had God's love in his heart, he wouldn't have been discouraged and been drinking. I hate Satan, Eric."

"OK, well, the next step is to ask God to forgive you and tell Him you're sorry for the mistakes you've made and that you want Him to accept you as His child," Eric explained.

"Is that all?" Susan asked. "Don't I have to do anything? I mean, like try to be good first or something?"

"No, I don't think so," Eric said thoughtfully. "That comes each day as you study and talk to God. He changes you and your faith in Him grow stronger."

"Wow, you really are smart! How do you know all this?"

"Oh, I just studied and talked to Kevin and everything. Are you ready to say the prayer now?"

The twins knelt down, each asking God to accept them as His children and to forgive them. They thanked Him for loving them. Then they got up and sat on Eric's bed.

"I don't feel any different," Susan commented.

"That's OK," Eric answered. "We've made a choice, and God counts that."

"Now what do we do, Eric?"

"We just start growing. I think we should read the Bible every day and talk to God about what we think and ask Him questions."

"You can share my Bible if you want to," Susan offered. "I'll leave it here on your desk, OK?" She twisted a corner of the bedspread around her finger. "Are you going to tell Aunt Myrtle about us being Christians? Do you think she'll laugh because we're only kids?"

"Nope, she won't." Eric spoke firmly. "I think she's been praying that we would learn to love God. Man, there are still so many things I'm not sure of. I hope I can understand them all."

"Susan! Eric!" Aunt Myrtle called up the stairs. "Let's go!"

They rode in silence until they reached the airport. Soon they found themselves struggling through the crowd behind Aunt Myrtle.

"Psst, Eric," Susan whispered. "Do you think Father will be angry?"

"I don't know, Susan. Let's not say anything about it until later, OK?"

"Hey, there he is!" Susan screamed. She ran to Father and threw her arms around him.

Eric walked slowly toward them. He was practically a man, and he wasn't about to look dumb like Susan did.

"Hello, Father," he said solemnly. Then forgetting himself, he grabbed his father in a big hug. Father loved them and would surely understand. Eric hoped so.

11

The Ugly Shell

Susan jumped out of bed. She pulled up the pink flowered sheet, smoothed out her ruffled spread, and plopped her pillow into place. Struggling into a baggy yellow shirt and white cotton pants, Susan brushed her hair back into a ponytail and tied it with a yellow ribbon. She ran to the window and gave the shade a yank. It snapped to the top of the window, flapping around several extra turns.

Susan settled herself among the soft, plump pillows on the window seat and peered out. Aunt Myrtle stood just below on the garden path, selecting pansies. She inspected each one, then placed it into the small basket that hung over one arm.

A small wisp of wind entered the garden, rippled past the swaying pampas grass, and lifted Aunt Myrtle's long brown curls, making them dance about. It fluttered through the ruffles on her flouncy blue dress, then caught up her straw hat and sent it tumbling down the garden path. Susan giggled to herself. Suddenly Dad appeared in the garden. He snatched up the hat and handed it to Aunt Myrtle. They both laughed.

He must have been watching too, Susan thought.

She got up and arranged the pillows, swished a brush through her bangs once more, then ran down the stairs and into the living room. Dad and Aunt Myrtle entered the room laughing.

"Why, princess. Good morning!" Dad caught her up in his arms. Susan felt a butterfly of happiness inside. Her dad seldom showed his affection so openly.

"I'm so glad you came, Dad!" She laughed.

"And where is that son of mine?" Dad teased.

"Holed up in a cave of warm blankets, dreaming about some adventure, I suspect," Aunt Myrtle said. Her eyes twinkled.

"I see he hasn't changed a bit. I'll see if I can't awaken the dreamer."

Susan heard him pound on Eric's door. *If only Dad knew just how much Eric has changed,* Susan mused, *what would he think*?

Soon they all sat around Aunt Myrtle's table in the kitchen, enjoying hotcakes topped with strawberries.

Eric thought of all the things he wanted to tell Dad— the trip to the tide pools, his sketch of Aunt Myrtle's couch, the new class at Sabbath School, and Dr. Foster.

"Well!" Dad laid his napkin on the table, pushed back his chair, and stood up. "I have an announcement."

Susan smiled up at Dad, admiring his brand-new shirt and tie. They looked expensive. Every hair on his head seemed in its place, and his black beard was perfectly formed against his face. She remembered how it had felt against her cheek when he'd hugged her earlier. He was handsome standing there. A little fear nibbled at her heart when she noticed that he still had the tired worry lines at the corners of his eyes. In fact, they seemed deeper than before.

"I want you all to know that, with the help of the police, my partner and I finally located that drunk who killed Mother."

Aunt Myrtle gasped. She didn't turn to face Dad.

"And I've slapped him into jail. I have a full confession of hit and run on him," Dad continued. He thumped his hand on the table. The glass dishes jumped. Susan saw a hard look fill Dad's eyes, and his jaw became rigid. Suddenly he looked like a mass of controlled rage.

"Do you know what that means, Myrtle?" Dad asked, turning to face Aunt Myrtle, who stood near the stove, spatula in hand.

"No, Frank, I'm not sure," she said in a low voice.

"It means that we'll be able to prosecute to the fullest. You know—stiff prison term and a fine to boot. That's one drunk who'll regret the day he opened a bottle."

Dad strode around the room. He pounded one fist into his open hand. All at once he flopped down into an empty chair. The room filled up with suffocating silence. Dad sat drumming his fingers on the table.

Susan stole a glance at Eric. He stared at his half-empty plate. She heard Aunt Myrtle scrape a singed pancake from the pan and toss it into the sink.

"Frank?" Aunt Myrtle's voice broke into the silence. She sat down beside him. "I know how important it has been for you to find the man whose irresponsible behavior cost Carol her life, but—"

"It hasn't been just important, Myrtle. It's been all I've thought about. I'm going to see that he pays plenty. His family too. They won't be able to live in the same town when I'm through with them."

"Frank!" Aunt Myrtle gasped. She placed a hand on his shoulder. "It seems to me that a person should be held responsible for his behavior. The man drove while intoxicated. He should be made to realize the terrible pain that he caused, but—"

"But what?" Dad demanded, his body tensing. Susan

saw the anger turn to pain.

"You've lost so much already, Frank. I don't want to see you lose yourself, also. The kids need you," she said, looking at Susan and Eric.

Dad glanced up at them as though just remembering they were in the room.

"That's exactly it, Myrtle. It's for them and for me."

"What do you mean, Dad will lose himself?" Susan blurted. She felt her whole body tense.

"Remember the summer we walked the shore of Assateague Island, Frank?"

"Yes, I remember." A softer look came into his eyes.

"I picked up a small round shell. The golden brown color seemed so lovely. But you said, 'It's an old moon snail. I hate those things. They have an awful habit.' "

"What habit, Dad?" Susan asked.

"I'm sure I'm about to fall into some sort of a lesson, Myrtle, but to answer your question, Susan, the moon snail is a predator. He makes a meal of any mollusk he finds. He's blind, but he feels his way as far as a foot beneath the sand, searching for food."

"But how can he open a clamshell to eat it, Dad?" Susan asked.

"For him it's easy. He clutches the poor victim in the grasp of his large fleshy foot and begins to drill a hole through the shell. The clam can't escape. Sooner or later the shell gives way, and the snail eats his fill."

Susan made a face. "It sounds awful!"

"Aunt Myrtle," Eric asked, "do you still have the moon snail? I'd like to see it."

"I certainly do. Just a minute." Aunt Myrtle hurried to her room and soon returned with the shell.

Eric took the moon snail in his hands. The brown coiled shell seemed harmless, even desirable. He looked at it for a moment and handed it to Dad.

"That was the summer I learned that some emotions can clutch at the heart and drill away at us until we are destroyed," Aunt Myrtle said. "When we are terribly hurt we want to hate—"

"Or take revenge. Is that it, Myrtle?" Dad's voice was tight.

"Yes, Frank. The worst of it is that anger and desire for revenge eat away at our peace and our very life. They can destroy us in the end."

"Why don't we just forgive that man?" Eric suggested. "I don't think I would feel very good knowing you were trying to hurt him, Dad."

"Oh, please do!" Susan pleaded. She sat down on Dad's lap.

"Get up, Susan, you're going to wrinkle my slacks."

Everyone stared at Dad.

"Eric, I can't believe what you just said. And you either, Susan. Why should I forgive the man who's wrecked my life?"

"It's just that—I—" Eric looked at Aunt Myrtle, asking silently for help.

"Because Jesus did," Susan said simply.

"That's right! Jesus forgave me for my sins, and He wants me to forgive others just like He always did. Even when He was on the cross, He forgave the ones who nailed Him there," Eric ended in a rush.

"Just a minute, Eric. Those are pretty fancy ideas. Just what sins has God forgiven you of that make you feel responsible to forgive others too?"

Eric saw Aunt Myrtle's encouraging smile.

"Well, I've been grumpy a lot and . . . I hated, too, Dad. Really I did. It made me miserable inside. I saw that very clearly one day in the tide pool. I saw my own glum face. I've even been selfish and mean."

"But he isn't so much anymore since—" Susan started, then clapped her hand over her mouth.

"Being grumpy and selfish—that doesn't seem like it calls for a lot of forgiveness," Dad said. He didn't smile at Eric.

"It doesn't matter how big or how little our sins are. They killed Jesus on the cross. They cost Him His life. I want Him to forgive me, so I have to forgive other people too. That's what He says."

"Did someone tell you that, Eric?" Dad demanded. He shot a look at Aunt Myrtle.

"No, Dad, I read it." Eric ran to his room and returned with an open Bible. He showed his dad the verse.

" 'Be ye kind one to another, tenderhearted, forgiving one another, even as God for Christ's sake hath forgiven you,' " Dad read aloud. He looked up at Eric. "Well! I see you've been doing some reading."

"Yes, Dad. I wanted my faith to grow stronger."

"Wait, Eric. I'm not sure what is going on here." He gave Aunt Myrtle another look.

When she smiled, her eyes twinkled.

"It's easy for you to talk about forgiveness—"

"Is it, Frank? I've been coming home to an empty house for twelve years because—" She stopped in mid-sentence. "I had to learn to forgive, Frank." She turned quickly. "You children get your things. We promised to show your dad some sights."

Eric stared at the two adults in amazement. The mystery was real! Just why did Aunt Myrtle live in an empty house? He wanted to know. But even more, he wanted Dad to stop allowing hate and anger to eat away at him. Like a moon snail, they had drilled their way into his very heart. He must find a way!

12

Strong Weaklings

S usan plodded along the dry sand. With a bare toe she lifted a broken clamshell from the sand and flipped it into the thin, foamy edge of a wave. A sea gull swished past unnoticed and landed with a splash in the water nearby.

For three days a whirl of activity had surrounded her. Then all too soon, Dad had boarded a plane and waved goodbye. The sleek craft grew smaller and smaller in the distance until it disappeared, leaving the sky and her heart empty.

She sat down on a rounded rock to think. So many questions tumbled around inside her. Why had Dad become so restless after that phone call from his partner? He'd visited the San Diego Zoo and Sea World and had gone on picnics with them, but he didn't seem to enjoy any of it. Several times she'd found him pacing the floor, deep in thought. And even though Eric and she had talked with him about their friends and activities, Dad never once mentioned his life or work in Maryland.

Susan sighed and scooped her fingers into the warm sand. She felt a hard, thin object and drew it out of the sand. When she brushed the sand from the almost flat surface, a delicate, five-petaled flower pattern looked up at her. It seemed almost as though someone had pricked .

it onto the shell with the tip of a knife blade.

Susan stood up and walked back to the house, stopping to look at the delicate shell from time to time.

"Aunt Myrtle, where are you?" she called, brushing the sand from her clothes and feet.

"I'm up here in the sewing room," a cheery voice answered.

"Look what I've found. It's so pretty. What is it?"

"So, you found an echinoderm." Aunt Myrtle laid the pink flowered cloth down beside the sewing machine and took the shell from Susan's hand.

"A what?"

"It's a sand dollar, Susan. You're lucky to find one that isn't broken."

"I can't imagine how a fragile shell like this ever lives in the sea. My fingers could easily smash this shell to bits."

"You're right. This shell is very weak. Yet it's perfectly suited for the life God gave it. Sand dollars burrow beneath the sand with little effort. They have an inner strength that you can't see. Let me show you." Aunt Myrtle opened a drawer, taking a sand dollar from a small box. She broke it into two pieces.

"Can you see the tiny pillars? They almost fill the space between the upper and lower shell. Sand dollars depend upon these internal pillars for safety and strength against the force of waves and also for burrowing into the sand. Live sand dollars are covered with tiny spines that help them move."

"You mean that it appears weak, but because of something inside, it is actually strong? That's neat!" Susan grinned appreciatively.

"That's right. God gives it the strength it needs to live in the dark, sandy world where He placed it."

Susan studied the sand dollar. She felt as weak as it looked. Even though she believed that Jesus loved her, her desire to do many things that she knew would hurt Him still bothered her. She still wanted to read novels and watch TV programs that even Mother had asked her not to see. Susan was still the same Susan as before, she mused. And Eric? He still complained a lot.

"Aunt Myrtle . . . what if . . . a person did decide to become a Christian? How would she become strong so that she could obey Jesus? I know some Christians who are still doing wicked things, and they don't obey God at all."

"That's true, Susan, but it doesn't need to be. You see, when Jesus forgives and accepts a person, He knows that it's impossible for that person to obey Him—or even want to. He knows that people are weak. That's why He wants to live within and give inner strength to His people just as He gave the sand dollar strength to live in the sand beneath the sea."

Susan poked at the sand dollar pieces with her finger. "What do you have to do to get Him to live inside and give you strength?"

"Susan, you don't understand. The desire to do right and the ability to obey are gifts from Jesus. He promises to change us so that we will become just like Him. We'll hate the things that we once loved so much. When we see our weakness it's good, because then Jesus is able to make us strong. Let me show you something."

Aunt Myrtle opened a small drawer and lifted a white ball of fluff from a blue box.

"This is cotton. It came right off a plant in a great cotton field that I visited in Louisiana several years ago."

Susan touched the soft, white fluff perched atop a

brown stem and ran her fingers over the hard, thin projections that divided the cotton into five sections. Large seeds hid inside the fluffy sections. Susan glanced at the bright material that lay beside the sewing machine. "This dress material is cotton, isn't it, Aunt Myrtle?"

"Yes. Isn't it wonderful to think that it came from a simple plant? Someone planned that that field of cotton should one day become a bolt of beautiful fabric."

"I know what you are going to say." Susan smiled at Aunt Myrtle. "Cotton can't become new dresses without some help."

Aunt Myrtle laughed. "It's even more than that. Cotton can't do anything but grow day by day under the sun and rain, rooted deep in the soil. The hands of trained men and machines make it into fabric for someone like me to create new dresses from."

Susan compared the cotton with the soft fabric. Suddenly she felt very much like talking with Aunt Myrtle about her decision to become a Christian. But she remembered her promise to Eric. If only he hadn't gone off on a camping trip with Kevin and Dr. Foster! Sad thoughts crowded into her mind. If only she'd been able to talk to Dad! But the right moment just never came, and now he had gone away. Susan looked up. Aunt Myrtle was looking at her, smiling in a way that made Susan wonder if Aunt Myrtle already knew about her decision.

"Susan, there's a promise that I like to remember often. You can find it in the book of Hebrews, chapter 4 and verse 16. Here's my Bible. Why don't you read it to me?"

Susan took the Bible and after some struggle located the verse.

" 'Let us therefore come boldly unto the throne of

grace, that we may obtain mercy, and find grace to help in time of need.' " Susan read the verse two times. She smiled at Aunt Myrtle. "Then God gives us help and victory?"

"Yes. There's a verse that says the very thing. Look at 1 Corinthians 15:57. It's in the New Testament."

" 'Thanks be to God, which giveth us the victory through our Lord Jesus Christ,' " Susan read. "God makes everything easy, doesn't He? He must want us to be able to grow to be like Him and not become discouraged."

"Even the strongest person is weak to do right. That's why God gives obedience and victory as gifts. We all depend upon that."

"I wish Dad could understand these things," Susan said wistfully. Her eyes filled up with tears that threatened to spill over her cheeks.

"I do too, Susan. Very much. We'll just have to keep on talking to God about him. And we need to remember that everyone has the choice to make. It isn't God's way to force or shame anyone into choosing Him."

Aunt Myrtle smiled. Her eyes twinkled with mischief. "Susan, take this piece of paper and pretend it is you. Now take this book and pretend that it stands for doing right."

Susan held the piece of paper in one hand and the heavy book in another.

"Now try to support the book with the paper," Aunt Myrtle encouraged.

Susan laughed. "I can't! The paper isn't strong enough to hold the book up."

"Aren't you even going to try?" Aunt Myrtle pretended to be shocked.

Susan laughed as she set the book on the edge of the

paper. As she expected, it just crashed to the floor. Aunt Myrtle handed her a stronger piece of paper, but it didn't support the book either.

"There's no way a Christian can have victory. God must do it for him. Now take this piece of white paper and roll your red piece up in it."

Susan rolled up the paper that represented her inside the white paper that represented Jesus.

"The only way a person can obey and change is to stay close to Jesus and receive His gift of obedience," Aunt Myrtle continued. She took three ribbons from a drawer.

"Let the first ribbon represent prayer. We stay close to Jesus by talking to Him about the things that we think about and that are important to us." Aunt Myrtle tied the blue ribbon around the rolled-up paper.

"What does the yellow ribbon represent?" Susan asked.

"It stands for reading and studying about God through nature and the Bible." Aunt Myrtle tied the yellow ribbon around the paper. Then she tied the third ribbon around the roll of paper with the others. "This stands for talking with others about our love for God—sharing. Now try to support the book on the paper."

Susan found it easy to balance the book on the column of rolled-up paper. The roll didn't come undone and cause the book to fall because the three ribbons held it firmly.

"Doing right is a heavy burden, just like this book, unless we're close to Jesus and allow Him to bear the weight. Then it's easy. He just does it for us. Our work is to stay wrapped up in Jesus and not let anything get us away from Him," Aunt Myrtle explained.

"May I keep the paper and ribbons?" Susan pleaded. "I want to show Eric when he comes home."

"Certainly, Susan. By the way, there's a wonderful Helper that Jesus has sent to make all this possible—"

A phone rang in the quiet morning. Aunt Myrtle smiled when she spoke to the voice on the other end of the line. "Sure she would . . . I'll tell her . . . fine . . . in ten minutes, then. Goodbye."

Aunt Myrtle turned from the phone. "Susan, that was Margo. She's coming by to visit for a while. How does a walk on the beach sound?"

"Super!" Susan shouted. "We'll build a huge sand castle, and —oh, what about the Helper you mentioned? Who is He?"

"You run along and build that castle. I think you need the exercise. We can finish our conversation later."

Aunt Myrtle smiled to herself as she watched the two girls skip out the door and into the sunshine. *There is one special child who is taking steps out of darkness and into new understanding. Thank You, Jesus!* She picked up the pink flowered material and began to sew.

13

Eyes for Susan

Margo and Susan bounded down the steps and flung themselves onto the warm, soft sand. They gazed up into the clear blue sky at fluffy clouds that drifted past on a lazy breeze.

"I'm glad you came by, Margo." Susan sat up, yanked off her shoes, and stuffed her socks into them. The girls let the fine white sand sift through their bare toes.

"Hey, let's feed the gulls," Margo suggested. She reached into her shirt pocket and pulled out a small plastic bag crammed full of dry bread pieces.

The girls began to throw the bread into the sky. Soon a tangled mass of white wings appeared overhead. The gulls swirled and swooped, pecking at each other in their haste to snatch up the tidbits.

When the last crumb had been tossed to the quarrelsome gulls, the girls decided to build a sand castle. They soon had sand in their hair and on their noses. It filtered into pockets and even into their ears. But the pile of shapeless sand had become a castle awaiting the arrival of a handsome prince.

Margo leaned back to admire their handiwork. "What were you and Aunt Myrtle talking about when I arrived?" she asked.

"Oh, something about a special helper that God sends

81

to be with us when we're trying to become like Jesus. I'm not sure who that could be. Aunt Myrtle said we would talk some more later." Susan scooped up a whole handful of dripping sand and let it fall with a plunk onto the castle wall.

"She must mean the Holy Spirit," Margo said, "Dr. Foster said that He . . . Hey, watch out!" she shouted.

Susan jerked around to see a small, frail-looking girl heading toward them. She was stumbling through the sand, arms outstretched, fingers clawing the empty air. Before Margo or Susan could scream out another warning, she caught a shabby tennis shoe in a hole and fell, face down, between them. She looked like a broken rag doll sprawled on top of the smashed castle.

"You stupid, clumsy—"

"Margo!" Susan gasped. "Are you all right?" she asked, reaching out to pull the girl to her feet. "Wow, you've got sand everywhere." Susan started to brush the wet sand from the girl's face and clothing.

"I—I just heard your voices. You sounded so happy."

"Who are you, anyway?" Margo's voice sounded harsh, and Susan saw her staring at the rumpled child.

"I'm Lisa. I live in the cottage on the hill," she said, turning toward Margo. "I'm sorry I scared you, but I—"

"You didn't scare us, you just ruined our sand castle, that's all. Can't you look where you're going?"

Susan noticed two tears spill from Lisa's vacant eyes and wash clean paths through the sand that clung to her cheeks. Suddenly she understood.

"You couldn't see us, could you?" Susan said gently. She gave Margo a fierce glance.

"I shouldn't have tried to find you," Lisa sobbed. She turned toward the sound of the waves crashing onto the beach and rubbed her wet hands together.

"Don't worry, Lisa. The water can't reach us here. How did you ever get down here from your house?" She took Lisa's thin hand in hers, and both girls sat down.

Lisa stopped crying. "Oh, I just fumbled around with the gate latch until it opened; then I followed the sound of your laughter. It was easy until—I heard the water."

"Does your mother know you are out here alone?" Margo asked. Her voice sounded softer.

"No! She'd skin me. Mother never lets me leave the house." A small smile teased the corners of her mouth. She brushed a blond curl from her eyes.

"We better help you get home," Susan suggested. "Your mother will be worried to pieces."

"I wish I could stay and play with you," Lisa begged. "I hate sitting alone in that dark old house."

"Well, how can you play? And besides it's dark out here for you too," Margo pointed out.

"But I can hear sounds and feel the wind and the sun. I could just sit nearby. I wouldn't be any trouble. Could I, please?"

"I know what we'll do," Susan announced. "Get up on my back. Let's go ask your mom if you can play. Margo and I can take you back home for supper."

Soon the three girls found themselves back on the beach. Lisa chattered all the way to the sea edge and allowed Susan to place her inside the walls of the castle.

"You are safe inside the castle. Feel the wall that surrounds it?"

Lisa ran her fingers along the smooth wall and laughed. "No wave can catch me in here!" she said as she began to pile up the sand and poke it with her fingers.

Margo and Susan repaired the walls of the castle. Waves crashed in the distance.

"Susan," Lisa called, "could you 'see' me to the edge of

the water? I want to touch it."

Susan cast Margo a questioning look. They looked at Lisa, who stood gazing with unseeing eyes at the water.

"Sure. We'll help you. Take our hands."

The three girls walked hand in hand to the water.

"Here comes a wave," Margo said.

"See it for me," Lisa pleaded, yanking on Susan's hand.

"You mean you've never seen a wave?" Margo asked.

"No. Please, see it for me!"

Susan stared at the wave building up before her. How could she help Lisa see it? She looked down at Lisa's expectant face and knew she had to try. "There is a great wall of green water out there," she began. "It piles up, up, up. Then it starts moving toward us. It's much taller than we are." Susan felt Lisa's hand tighten in hers.

"Now it's just standing still for a second, the thin edge quivering. Here it comes tumbling down the front side of itself with lots of bubbles and foam. The wave is getting shorter and shorter and very bubbly."

"I hear it!" shouted Lisa. "I want to touch it."

"Hang on tight!" Susan screamed. "Now, Margo, lift her up."

Margo and Susan lifted Lisa up over the wild, churning water and let her feet dangle in its wildness. She screamed out her delight.

"Now the water will run up onto the sand and return to the sea," Susan explained.

They let Lisa feel the water rush past and trickle back over her feet on its way to the sea. She begged to stay again and again as the waves played tag with the sand. At last Susan and Margo fell, exhausted. They carried Lisa home and knocked on the cottage door. A tired, thin woman in a faded blue dress opened the door.

"Mother, Mother, I saw the waves! I tasted the salty water, and my toes touched the bubbles! Susan 'saw' them for me. It felt wonderful!"

Margo and Susan waved goodbye and started off down the path. They hooked the gate latch and turned toward the cottage. Lisa and her mother stood waving.

"Please come again, girls," Lisa's mother called.

"Please come back. 'See' for me, Susan," Lisa called.

"We will, we will," Margo and Susan shouted. They ran all the way to Aunt Myrtle's house and bounded up the steps into the kitchen.

"Aunt Myrtle!" Susan shouted. "We 'saw' for a blind girl. We helped her feel the water and 'see' a wave."

"What's this?" Aunt Myrtle asked, entering the kitchen. She sat down and motioned the girls to sit beside her at the table. The whole story spilled out with happy words tumbling together into the warm kitchen.

"How wonderful!" Aunt Myrtle exclaimed. "Now, Susan, you and Margo have just experienced what the Holy Spirit does every time He helps someone."

"What do you mean?" Margo asked. "What does a blind girl have to do with the Holy Spirit?"

"A lot, Margo." Aunt Myrtle picked up her Bible. "You see, we're a bit blind about some things too. Like understanding the Bible and knowing what God wants us to do. The Holy Spirit actually—"

"He sees for us, that's what He does!" Susan shouted. She jumped up and twirled about the room.

"Yes," Margo said. "Just like we 'saw' for Lisa. Wow! That's neat."

"Show us in the Bible," Susan asked, pulling up a chair next to Aunt Myrtle.

"First of all, the Holy Spirit is one of the Beings of the Trinity. He helped God and Jesus create the world. You can read about that in Genesis 1:2."

Susan located the verse and read the words, "The Spirit of God moved upon the face of the waters."

"He's responsible for helping us see and understand the Bible. He guided the prophets in writing the Bible, and now He's our helper in understanding the verses and in becoming like Jesus," Aunt Myrtle explained.

"I heard something about fruits of the Spirit once," Margo said. "What are those?"

"When the Holy Spirit lives in the heart, with our permission, of course, He brings love, joy, peace, patience, kindness, goodness, faithfulness, gentleness, and self-control. They are the result of His living in us."

"Wow!" Susan gasped, "I could use some of those."

"So could I," Margo admitted. She remembered her harsh words to Lisa.

Susan thought about Lisa stumbling in the darkness, afraid and lonely, wanting to see the waves. "There can be a darkness inside us, in our minds," Aunt Myrtle explained. "We need the Holy Spirit to bring us light and to be our eyes—the eyes of our understanding, as it were. Do you understand that?" She looked at the girls.

"We sure do," Margo answered.

The kitchen door burst open, and Eric walked in. His blond hair stood on end, and his shirt was torn and dirty. Both shoelaces hung limp and untied. He flashed them a grin and dropped his pack on the clean floor. "I'm home and I'm hungry, and I have a million things to tell you that you'll never believe!" He brushed the unruly shock of hair from his eyes when he saw Margo.

"What a day," Dr. Foster sighed, shoving Eric's bedroll inside.

Yes, what a day, Susan thought. What a wonderful day!

14

Eric's Poriferan

Eric stooped down and unzipped his pack. He pulled out a small Ziploc bag and plopped it down on the kitchen table in front of Aunt Myrtle.

"I brought you something," he said, pointing to several thin red objects that sloshed about in a murky liquid.

"Oh, yuck! What's that?" Susan wrinkled up her nose and poked at the bag with her finger.

"Hey! I almost drowned myself scraping that stuff off a rock so I could bring it home. That isn't yuck, it's some poriferan." Eric glanced up at Aunt Myrtle to catch her reaction. When her eyes filled with a pleased look, he gave Susan a see-how-smart-I-am look.

"Why, Eric, you're absolutely right!" Aunt Myrtle said, peering into the bag at the red objects.

"Poriferan! What are they?" Susan asked.

"They're sponges," Eric said importantly. "This one is a velvety red encrusting sponge. I found it attached to an overhanging rock in a crevice almost a foot beneath the surface. They grow along the California coast and can be seen when the tide is quite low, exposing creatures at the middle tide zone." He drew in a deep breath and looked at Susan with a smug expression.

"That's a sponge?" She opened the bag carefully and

took out one of the smooth pieces. "Look at all those starlike openings. It's strange."

Aunt Myrtle laughed. "You're just used to sponges shaped more like round balls or long tubes. The velvety red sponge is an encrusting type that grows a bit like moss."

"Some plant!" Eric said.

"Actually, Eric, this is an animal. There's a whole community of individual cells living together. Each has an individual function."

Susan and Eric stared at Aunt Myrtle and then at the sponge that sat in a pool of water on the table.

"If you will bring me the yellow ball-like object from the windowsill in my room, Eric, I'll show you something interesting."

Eric soon returned with a fluffy-looking ball. Holes and openings cluttered its surface.

"That looks more like a sponge," Susan said.

"This sponge has a whole system of canals surrounded by cells," Aunt Myrtle explained. "Water is pumped through them with the help of tiny swishing cilia hairs. As the water passes through the chambers, sticky funnel-shaped collar cells trap food. The flow of water also brings in oxygen and takes away waste."

"Wow!" Susan gasped. "How strange."

"This sponge had microscopic glasslike splinters called spicules inside it that acted as a skeleton. It felt sharp and hard and was quite useless until it was properly treated."

"It still feels too rough to be used." Susan squeezed the sponge between her fingers. "I wouldn't want to run that over my skin."

"This sponge is like people. Let's say a person decides to become a Christian." Aunt Myrtle looked straight at the twins. "They would then belong to God and choose to live differently, just like this sponge belongs to me and has been treated so that it is no longer a creature living in the sea but is now useful to help me. We call that conversion, or change in purpose. That's not enough. Something has to happen every day—"

The ringing phone interrupted her. "That's got to be Kevin," Eric said. "We're going surfing. That is, if it's OK with you, Aunt Myrtle."

"Go ahead, Eric. And tell that scamp Kevin hello for me. He'll make a water bug out of you yet!"

"I can go. It's all settled," Eric shouted into the phone.

Susan felt surprised to see Eric so excited. Before she could even tease him, he had rummaged in his pack, grabbed a towel and swimsuit, and fled out the door.

"Aunt Myrtle," Susan said, fidgeting with the sponge, "would you tell me about what has to happen every day for the sponge to be useful?"

"Get me a large pan of water," Aunt Myrtle instructed.

Susan filled a pan with water and placed it on the table.

Aunt Myrtle picked up the sponge. "I own this sponge. No one can take it as his own, since it belongs to me. But before it can be useful, I have to keep it wet and soft. Dip it into the water, Susan."

Susan poked a corner of the sponge into the water.

"More than that. Most of the sponge is still hard and useless."

Susan plunged the sponge under the water, then pulled it out. The outer edges dripped water and felt soft. But when she squeezed it, the inside still felt hard and inflexible.

"It's going to take even more than that," Aunt Myrtle said with a smile. "Squeeze it hard."

Susan held the sponge beneath the water for several moments. As she squeezed it, she felt it become very soft and flexible. The sponge could hold a lot of water, but after just so much, the water poured from it and landed with a splash in the pan.

"Now it's ready for service," Aunt Myrtle announced. "Can you figure out how people are like that?"

Susan thought for a minute. She stared at the sponge. "I think so," she said slowly. "I'm like the sponge. I belong to Jesus. He has 'treated' me so that the sharp, ugly things like spicules are gone—or at least are going away. I am changed. Now I choose to live differently." She hesitated.

"Go on. That's right so far," Aunt Myrtle encouraged.

"He wants me to become useful and work for Him. So every day I need to—what does the squeezing in water mean?"

"Do you remember that Jesus said He was the Water of Life?"

"Oh, now I know! I must take in the water like this sponge. I need Jesus in my life every day. I have to be full of thoughts of Him. But how do you take Jesus into your life?" Susan's face puckered into a frown.

"By reading the Bible, talking to God about your needs and about how you feel, and studying Him in nature."

"I know!" Susan said, jumping about the room. "Then I share with others and squeeze out all that love that I have taken inside." She filled the sponge with water and squeezed it out. "I need to be filled with Jesus *all* the time, don't I?" she asked. "So that's why I don't feel very good when I just have a quick prayer and read for only a few minutes!" Before Aunt Myrtle could agree with her, she admitted, "I get in such a hurry."

Aunt Myrtle's eyes shone bright with understanding.

Susan felt relieved. "I guess I'll go to my room for a while," she said.

Susan spent the afternoon in her room. She struggled to write out a schedule for the days ahead. *I guess I need more time at night to study my Sabbath School lesson,* she thought. She got her Bible, lesson quarterly, and a book, *The Desire of Ages,* and placed them in a drawer of the night stand. "Now I'm ready. Next, how am I going to squeeze out some of this love to someone else?" she asked herself.

Susan heard Eric come in and slam his door. She listened as he struggled with a piece of furniture. He dragged it out of his room and thumped it down the stairs. She realized he was headed for the storage shed when she heard the kitchen door slam behind him. She wished he had time to sit and talk with her. Just how could she share—and with whom?

She sat at her desk and doodled and tapped her pencil, just like she had seen Aunt Myrtle do when she was thinking. No idea popped into her empty head. At last she decided to talk to God about it. She walked to the window and looked out. The warm, clear day looked inviting. *What a day to build a sand castle,* she thought. "That's it!" she shouted. "Lisa! I'll share some of the stories about Jesus and His miracles with her. She can't read them for herself." Susan danced around the room. Suddenly her door opened, and Eric's head peeked in. He stared at her.

"What are you doing in here?" he asked. "You're sure making a lot of racket."

"Me? I thought *you* were tearing the whole house down a while ago. What have you been doing?"

"Just doing some investigating," Eric teased.

"Investigating what?"

"Some old letters." Eric pretended to be bored with the whole conversation.

"So that's where you've been. In the storage shed, snooping," Susan accused. She placed her hands on her hips and scowled at him.

"You don't even want to know what I found?" Eric said, looking surprised.

"Who cares about a bunch of old letters?" Susan retorted.

"Nobody, I guess. They were just sent to Aunt Myrtle by an old boyfriend anyway."

"Aunt Myrtle! She had a boyfriend? Hurry up, tell me what they said! Who was he?"

"I'd call that interest," Eric teased. He flopped onto the floor in front of Susan's window. Susan sat down beside him.

"I didn't really read the letters," Eric admitted. "I just had time to scan them. The guy—whoever he was—just signed them Sailor Boy. How dumb! He said he was going to marry Aunt Myrtle, and they would watch the sea through the window in the observation room every day. It got kind of mushy, so I skipped the rest of that one."

"I wonder why this guy didn't marry her," Susan said. "Aunt Myrtle is so much fun. And she's pretty too."

"Yeah," Eric agreed. "He sure was dumb. Aunt Myrtle must have really liked him since she never married anyone else." Eric thought about that for a long time. "And to think, she even let me take her special observation room," he said at last.

Susan and Eric sat quietly as the sunlight that danced on the windowsill grew dimmer. Their thoughts suddenly screeched to a halt at the sound of a loud *thump, thump* on the door.

15

The Surprise

Susan jumped to her feet, startled by a loud knock on her bedroom door.

"Who is it?" she asked, opening the door just enough to peek out.

"A wild gorilla who is about to eat you," boomed a voice.

"Oh, it's you, Dr. Foster." Susan giggled. "Come in."

"Looks like I found two in one. Hello, Eric."

"Hello, sir," Eric said. He stood up and grasped Dr. Foster's large hand. Eric felt warm all over. He liked the way Dr. Foster made him seem important.

"I know you two are busy with all sort of things during these summer months, but I wonder if you could give me a hand for a couple of weeks."

"Sure we can, can't we, Susan?" Eric gave Susan a small nudge. "What kind of help do you need?"

"I need a couple of responsible people who would straighten up my office and clean up some equipment for me. Twice a week for about three hours would do it, I think."

"Hey, that would be fun," Eric said. "When do we start?"

"If you don't mind, I would like to take you over to the office right now and show you around. After that, I'm taking your Aunt Myrtle out to dinner. Think you two could manage a meal at home on your own tonight?" Dr. Foster gave the twins a mischievous wink.

"Myrtle," Dr. Foster called. He started down the stairs with the twins right behind. "I just located my rescue team. We're going to the office for a bit. See you for dinner at five."

Aunt Myrtle smiled and followed them out to Dr. Foster's Jeep.

"Listen!" Susan commanded, stopping suddenly.

Eric almost fell over her. He was about to grumble about her careless ways when the sounds of joyous singing reached him.

"It's coming from the beach. Let's go see who's singing," Susan pleaded. "It's so beautiful."

"Hey, we have work to do," Eric protested.

"I think we could spare a minute, don't you, Eric?" Dr. Foster asked.

Susan scrambled down the steps to the beach. The others followed close behind. A group of people stood down by the wet sand. A tall man with gray hair stood facing a boy about Eric's height. They both wore black robes. A breeze caught their long wide sleeves and whipped them about. Another gust of wind blew itself into their robes and billowed them out like two balloons about to become airborne.

Suddenly the people began to sing again. The man and boy edged their way into the surf, struggling through the frothy edges of a wave. They stood just beyond the wildest water. The man raised one arm into the air and spoke a few words. Before Eric could ask Aunt Myrtle what she thought the words might be, the man had plunged the boy beneath the water. The boy burst to the surface, and the two of them struggled toward shore before an incoming wave could catch them.

"What was that all about?" Eric asked, watching the people crowd around the soaking-wet boy.

"You just witnessed a baptism, Eric," Aunt Myrtle said. "A beautiful one at that."

"These people were imitating a pattern set up by Jesus hundreds of years ago. Evidently this young man made a decision to become a Christian and be baptized," Dr. Foster explained.

Susan and Eric exchanged nervous glances. "That's great," Eric mumbled, "but why did he have to get dunked under the water in front of all these people?"

"Why did they come out here for the baptism instead of just sprinkling the guy with some water in church?" Susan asked before anyone could answer Eric's question.

"Good questions!" Dr. Foster said. He flashed Aunt Myrtle a grin. "The Bible teaches that when a person realizes he needs forgiveness for his sins and wants to live a new life patterned after the life of Jesus, he makes this desire known to others by following the example of Jesus. It is a public statement, and the baptism itself represents cleansing from sin and joining the family of God," Dr. Foster explained.

"The word *baptism* means to plunge or immerse, Susan," Aunt Myrtle added.

"But does a person have to be baptized like that in public?" Eric hated the thought of all the people staring at him. If he slipped or something, they might even laugh. It just didn't seem very important. Wasn't the important thing that he became a Christian?

"Maybe baptism is a way of showing we have learned the truth about God and want to follow Him," Susan suggested. "If God asked someone to do something that seemed hard for them to do, wouldn't He help them?"

"Certainly He would," Dr. Foster agreed. "I don't know if that boy felt afraid, but I'm sure that if he did, God was right there helping him to witness to the people watching."

"I think they were singing to encourage the boy and to praise God that he had made a good choice. I didn't notice laughing, even when he struggled with that long robe," Aunt Myrtle added.

"They're leaving now," Susan observed. She pointed to the group of people who talked and laughed as they wrapped the boy in a blue blanket.

"Let's be on our way." Dr. Foster headed for the Jeep. They waved goodbye to Aunt Myrtle and started down the winding road.

"You didn't tell us what the man said to the boy when he raised his hand," Eric reminded.

"He probably said something like this, Eric. 'I now baptize you in the name of the Father, and the Son, and the Holy Spirit.' "

"Those are the beings of the Trinity," Susan said. "Aunt Myrtle explained them to us."

"Another interesting thing about baptism is that it represents our death to an old way of life, our burial of that old life, and our being raised again into a new life with Jesus. The Lord has given us lots of symbolic things that help remind us of Him."

The twins thought about Dr. Foster's words and the baptism they'd just seen. Eric wanted to see Dr. Foster's office, but he just couldn't stop thinking about the boy in the surf. He looked at Susan. She seemed to be struggling with thoughts of her own.

Silence crept into the Jeep and filled every corner. Dr. Foster glanced in the twins' direction several times, but he didn't say anything. Susan and Eric lost track of the turns Dr. Foster made. Finally, Eric whispered in Susan's ear. Susan smiled and nodded her head. The twins looked up at Dr. Foster.

"I suppose that if a person decided to be a Christian, it would be—"

"We accepted Jesus as our Saviour," Susan blurted. "Days ago. In Eric's room."

"I showed her about the prayer of acceptance and forgiveness," Eric explained before Dr. Foster could say a word.

"What are you two knobby heads saying?" Dr. Foster questioned. He brought the Jeep to a screeching stop at the side of the road.

"We want to be baptized," Susan explained. "Like the boy."

"Yeah," Eric agreed.

The twins looked at the surprise written all over Dr. Foster's face as he studied them for a moment. "You are serious, aren't you?" he said finally. Dr. Foster rumpled Eric's hair with a big hand and flipped one of Susan's braids. Then he grabbed the steering wheel and started the Jeep.

"Where are you going?" Eric protested.

Dr. Foster whistled softly as he sped over the road. In just a minute they arrived at Aunt Myrtle's door.

"Out with you," he ordered, waving his hand. "Myrtle, come out here," Dr. Foster shouted.

Aunt Myrtle opened the door. She clutched a wad of papers in her hand.

"These two rascals just told me they gave their lives to Jesus days ago and didn't say a word to anyone."

The twins looked expectantly at Aunt Myrtle.

16

The Broken Law

A unt Myrtle smiled down into Susan and Eric's upturned faces, her eyes lingering for a moment on each with a silent, searching look that seemed to reach right inside their minds.

"Aren't you surprised that we decided to become Christians?" Susan asked at last. Her voice dripped with disappointment. This quiet lady with the serious eyes just didn't match the spontaneous Aunt Myrtle she'd come to know.

Aunt Myrtle held out her arms. "Come here, kids."

Eric noticed a suspicious moistness in her eyes. He felt confused. Suddenly he realized just how much he really wanted to please this aunt he'd come to love. He glanced at Dr. Foster, who gave him an encouraging nod, then joined Susan as she received a warm hug. It felt good, but he acted as untouched by it as possible.

"I'm not surprised, you rascals!" Aunt Myrtle held them at arm's length as though to get a better look at them. "I'm very happy!" She smiled her brightest smile, and Eric felt good inside.

"You see," Aunt Myrtle explained, "I've seen you grow-ing toward this day by day, just as I've watched many a struggling plant grow and bloom at last."

Dr. Foster threw his head back and laughed a warm

and hearty laugh that Susan thought would fill the whole sky. "Never knew anyone who could hide anything important from you, Myrtle." He looked at Aunt Myrtle with talking eyes. It seemed to Susan that time stood still.

"Hey! Aren't we going to see your office today?" Eric interrupted the silence.

"Uh—yes," Dr. Foster said, prying his eyes off Aunt Myrtle's face. "Into the Jeep with you two." He waved his hands at the twins, turned and smiled at Aunt Myrtle, then jumped into the driver's seat.

Before long they arrived at Dr. Foster's office and entered a large room neatly arranged with soft chairs and several tables. A painting of a fluffy white dog romping with a small boy nearly filled one wall.

"This room will need regular cleaning and rearranging so that it looks like this," Dr. Foster explained, directing their eyes with a sweep of his hands. "Things can get pretty shabby by the end of a busy day. My patients don't always have the best of manners."

Susan tried to memorize the arrangement of the room and where each magazine was placed. She noticed that Eric studied the room carefully also. She could just imagine how it looked and sounded when it was full of dogs and cats with their owners struggling to keep everything straight. She clamped her hand over her mouth, barely catching a giggle that threatened to escape.

"This is the examination room," Dr. Foster continued. He explained how he wanted the shelves to be cleaned and arranged. The twins paid close attention to his instructions. They didn't want anything to go wrong when they took care of this mysterious room filled with bottles and instruments.

Susan knew he expected everything to be shiny and

clean. The room fairly glowed, and the examining table looked spotless.

Eric looked around the room, imagining himself in a long white coat, striding about giving careful instructions to his patients' owners. He could almost hear their profuse thanks for the excellent surgery he'd performed that had undoubtedly saved the lives of their beloved pets.

". . . and I think you might enjoy helping me with some minor surgery as soon as you have a chance to get used to the routine and rules of my office, Eric." Dr. Foster's words jarred Eric from his thoughts.

"Wow, I would like that!" Eric grinned.

Susan could almost reach out and touch the excitement that filled the room. Eric sure liked the idea of working with Dr. Foster. Susan had to admit it was nice to see Eric excited about something.

Dr. Foster showed them how to measure the cleaning liquids and where to stow everything away when they'd finished. Then they piled into the Jeep and started off toward Aunt Myrtle's house.

"You sure have a lot of rules about your office," Susan observed. "I hope I can remember them and do everything right."

"I know I do, Susan. But I've found that things go better in the office if I follow guidelines. I ask my patients' owners to follow them also. Rules are important to protect not only ourselves but others as well. Take traffic laws, for instance." Dr. Foster pointed. "Look, we're about to start down a sharp incline. See this sign?" Dr. Foster indicated a yellow sign to their right.

"It says to reduce speed to twenty-five miles per hour," Eric said. "That looks like several tight curves ahead of us."

"You're right, Eric." Dr. Foster slowed down and started into the first turn. They made their way easily around the curve. Dr. Foster glanced into the rearview mirror. He frowned. "That guy is coming much too fast. He'd better slow down."

"He's right on your bumper," Eric warned, turning to watch the yellow convertible that had come up behind them with a roar. The driver honked angrily, urging them to speed up or get out of the way.

"Can't we go faster?" Susan worried. "I don't like that car following so closely behind us."

"No, Susan. The turns are much too sharp. That's why there is a law to go twenty-five miles an hour. It's there to protect us. That guy is in too big a hurry for his own—"

At that moment the driver of the yellow car gunned his motor and edged by them. He roared around the corner, honking his horn in irritation and shaking his fist. "Drive it or park it!" he shouted. A girl sat beside him. Eric could see her blond hair whipping in the wind. She laughed at them.

Eric glanced at Dr. Foster. He didn't see any anger in Dr. Foster's eyes, only sadness.

Suddenly the air was filled with the sound of screeching brakes and crunching metal. A cloud of dust billowed into the air. Eric could hear a smashing, like trees being broken, and the terrible sound of a woman screaming.

"Oh no!" Dr. Foster groaned. He brought the Jeep to a stop as far off the road as he could. "You two stay right here! Flag down the next car that comes along and tell the passengers to call an ambulance and the police. I'm going down to see if I can help." Dr. Foster climbed over the twisted pieces of guardrail and disappeared down the steep bank.

Eric wanted to follow Dr. Foster, yet he didn't dare. Someone needed to stay with Susan, who was close to tears, and someone had to flag a car down for help. The whole world seemed to scream out its silence. Long minutes passed. No car came along. Dr. Foster didn't reappear at the top of the embankment. There was nothing Eric and Susan could do but wait.

After what seemed like forever, Dr. Foster climbed onto the road. He wiped his forehead with a dirty, torn sleeve, then walked to the Jeep and leaned against it before climbing inside. His body slumped against the steering wheel, and a groan escaped from deep down inside him.

After a while, Eric said, "No one came along to flag, Dr. Foster. Are the people hurt badly down there?"

"The car—it looked like a towel someone had wrung the water from and tossed aside. There was nothing I could do. The two young people are—both dead." He looked at the shocked twins, then started up the Jeep and edged onto the road. "We'll just have to stop and phone the police. There is nothing else we can do. If only they had obeyed the laws that were there to protect them. If only . . ."

When they arrived at home, Dr. Foster told Aunt Myrtle the whole sad story.

"You know," Aunt Myrtle said at last, "laws are so often thought of as enemies. But they're really our friends. I do wish there weren't something called sin inside us that seems to propel us toward escaping the protection of law. We even fight God's special laws, and we pay the consequences. It makes me so sad."

"Does God have special protection laws?" Susan asked in a quiet voice. "Can you show them to me?"

"There are ten of them, Susan. They cover our love for

God and our love for one another. They are guides on how we should behave and live. You can find them in the book of Exodus, chapter 20."

Eric and Susan took a Bible off Aunt Myrtle's table and read the whole chapter. They looked up with serious faces.

"These look pretty hard to obey," Eric said.

"They would be," Dr. Foster agreed, "except that Christ gives us the power to obey, as well as the desire. He gave us these laws only to keep us from pain and sorrow."

"We obey them because we love Him," Susan said. She walked to the window and looked out. "If the people in the car had obeyed, they wouldn't be—" A sob escaped Susan's throat.

Aunt Myrtle moved toward her quickly.

"I'm sorry this whole thing happened, children," Dr. Foster said soberly. "Perhaps we can remember it as a warning to us. When we refuse to follow the laws made to protect us, we often suffer in ways God didn't intend for us to ever suffer. He only wants our lives to be happy and patterned after His. If it hurts us to see people suffer, just think how much it hurts God. He loves much more than we do."

"I'm sorry for being such a baby," Susan sniffed. "Isn't it almost five o'clock? You and Aunt Myrtle are still going out, aren't you?" Susan looked at Dr. Foster, who looked at Aunt Myrtle.

"After this afternoon, we'd understand if you didn't want to be left alone. We can go another time," Dr. Foster suggested.

"We'll be OK," Eric said. He looked at Susan and knew she felt just like he did. He knew she just wanted some quiet time to think and maybe study the ten laws they had discovered.

17
Pagurus

S usan listened to the last sounds of Dr. Foster's Jeep as it sped out the driveway and down the road. She slumped back against a plump pillow, drew her legs up, and tucked her toes beneath the edge of her soft blanket.

The last gentle rays of sunlight lingered on the windowsill. Susan listened. The distant crash of surf against the sand suddenly made her restless.

"Let's go for a walk before dark," she called to Eric.

Soon they found themselves running along the sea's edge, laughing at the tiny sanderlings that scurried along the waves' fringes. Their tiny legs moved so quickly that they looked like small windup toys let loose from a child's hand. Tiny bills jabbed into the wet sand as they hurried along in bunches like clouds blown across the sky by a gust of wind.

Soon the twins reached the tide pools where miniature crabs darted about and seaweed flowed in and out with the undulation of the water. Susan and Eric peered into the pools and laughed at the tiny fish that darted behind ledges to hide from their monster faces.

"Look!" Susan shouted. "Pagurus!"

"Who?" Eric asked, leaning his face so close to the water that an incoming wavelet sloshed over his head.

He jumped up, shaking his wet hair and coughing. Susan laughed so hard she almost fell into the pool herself. "Pagurus, the hermit crab," she said between giggles.

"Let's catch him!" Eric smoothed his wet hair back and looked out to sea to gauge the next wave before he tried to take another look into the pool. The water steadied in the pool, and soon he could see clearly. But no crab appeared.

"There isn't anyone there," he complained to Susan. Eric swished his arm about the pool to scare up the crab. The pool revealed nothing alive that resembled a crab.

Susan waited until a wave rushed its skirts over the pool and retreated. "There he is!" she shouted, pointing into the water.

"There's nothing there but an old black turban shell," Eric grumbled. "You and your crab."

"That's him! He lives in that shell. Grab him, Eric!"

Eric plunged his arm into the pool and came up with a shiny black shell. An orange, furry-looking crab protruded from the opening of the shell. It had two black-and-yellow-striped eyes that stuck out on the end of long stalks. The crab tried to retreat but couldn't pull all of itself into the shell.

"He didn't build a large enough shell to hide in," Eric said. "That wasn't too smart, fella," he said to the crab, who waved a large claw at him.

"It isn't his house. He borrowed it. Looks like he needs to find a larger one. Maybe he was looking for one when we found him."

"You mean he has to find a new shell when he grows too large for the one he lives in?" Eric asked, amazed.

"That's right!" Susan answered. "Hey, let's try to get him to move out of this one. Here is a wavy top shell. It's larger." Susan plopped the shell into a shallow pool, and Eric put the hermit crab nearby. They stayed out of sight the best they could and waited and watched. Nothing happened for a long time.

After what seemed like forever, the crab unfolded the large crusher claws that it used to block its house entrance and moved toward the wavy top shell. It waved small antennae and touched the shell. The crab turned the shell over and felt all over it with the antennae, even poking inside it. Then suddenly, almost faster than the twins could see, it popped out of the small shell and whirled around, stuck the soft part of its body into the wavy top shell, and backed in. It pulled all the way inside and covered the entrance with its large claws.

"Wow!" Eric exclaimed. He tapped on the shell and shook it, but Pagurus didn't come out. "Come out of there; I want to get another look at you," Eric commanded.

The crab didn't budge.

"Why do you think he is called a hermit crab?" Susan teased. "He isn't a bit interested in whether you know him or not. You might as well give up."

Eric held the shell up a moment, then let it fall with a plop into the pool. "That's just the way God seems to me sometimes," he grumbled. "He doesn't seem to be very easy to know, either."

"I think God does want us to know Him and understand what He's doing," Susan disagreed. "That's why He gave us prophets. God tells them, and their job is to tell us His messages. Aunt Myrtle says there have always been prophets during the years of this world's history."

"Well, that may be true for the Bible days, but there

aren't any now. The Bible prophets don't talk about things I'm interested in."

"That's why God did give us a prophet for our times. I think He knew it would be hard for us to figure out all the answers we needed. He was being extra helpful because He wants us to be happy."

"A prophet for now?" Eric asked. He wrinkled his forehead.

"Sure. You read one of her books last week—*Happiness Digest*," Susan said.

"Now, how do you know the lady who wrote that book was a prophet like the Bible prophets? Anyway, she was a woman. Prophets are always men."

"No, they aren't," Susan argued. "In Paul's time there were four ladies who were prophets. You can read about them in Acts 21."

"Well, I did like the book, and I figured that Ellen White must know a lot to write it, but how can you know who is a prophet and who isn't? Anyone could claim to be a messenger for God."

Susan looked into the pool a while before answering.

"I think we need to test what they say by the other Bible prophets. They should all agree. And their lives should show they know God. Ellen White became God's messenger when she was only seventeen. Aunt Myrtle said that she has written lots of books to help people know and love God. God isn't like a hermit crab who hides from us and doesn't want to know him."

"You're convinced that this lady is a real prophet?" Eric still looked doubtful.

"Yes. I read a book called *His Messenger*. It helped me apply the Bible test to her life and words. You can borrow it from Aunt Myrtle if you like. You'll be amazed at the miracles that happened when she received information from God to share with us. She didn't breathe at all while He was talking to her but was very much alive. She had strength to hold a heavy Bible in one hand while she turned the pages to read texts, except she didn't even look at the texts. She looked toward heaven. I wish I could have been there to see it."

Eric poked about in the seaweed and thought about what Susan said. He really did want to understand what God wanted him to do. He thought about how hard he struggled to obey God. The pressure was getting him down. Now that everyone knew he had made his decision to be a Christian, it seemed even harder. He started writing down all the things he didn't want to do anymore and all the things he should do. It didn't help. He felt angry at God. Now Susan was telling him one more thing. If God gave a prophet who wrote so many books, they might be full of more things that he couldn't do. It surprised him that Susan seemed happy about all this. She didn't seem troubled at all.

"Another way you can tell whether a prophet is from God," Susan continued, "is by seeing whether his prophecies come true all the time."

"Maybe so," Eric grumbled. "I guess I have to admit that God is trying to talk to us. I want to check it out for myself, though. Let's go now. It's getting dark."

They picked their way around the pools and ran up the beach to the house. A delivery truck sat near the back door. A man jumped out of the truck. He held a large vase of red roses in one hand. "This is for the lady of the house."

Eric and Susan stared at the small card that peeked from the mass of red flowers. Two words jumped out at them: *Sailor Boy*. They gasped and stared at each other.

After twelve years the mystery man had reappeared!

Suddenly they heard the sound of Dr. Foster's Jeep coming up the road. They turned and walked silently into the house.

18

Taught by a Fish

D r. Foster eased his lanky frame out of the Jeep. "Hi, kids!" He grinned. He rumpled Eric's hair with his hand and gave Susan's braided ponytail a flip that sent it swishing about. Then he followed Aunt Myrtle and the twins into the kitchen.

"Roses!" Aunt Myrtle exclaimed when she saw the vase sitting on the table. She buried her face in the soft blooms, breathing deeply, then glanced at Dr. Foster. Eric couldn't tell what the glance meant. He suddenly wished he had left the card sticking out where Aunt Myrtle might have seen it more easily and known who left the flowers.

"Sailor Boy has to be Dr. Foster," Eric whispered to Susan after everyone had said good night and he and Susan had gone to his room to talk. "He loves the ocean just like she does."

"But he hasn't been around here for twelve years," Susan protested. "Unless, of course, he moved away and returned for some reason. Who knows?" she groaned.

The twins stood looking out the large window at the crashing waves for a long time. They talked about their letters from Dad. He seemed so busy. He hadn't mentioned coming for another visit nor given them a date when he'd be able to move west to be with them. Susan wanted to ask Eric about the book she'd seen him push under his bed but instead she sighed and said good night.

Eric watched her open his door and walk out. He could hear her singing a bouncy little tune as she prepared for bed. A long silence followed; then her light blinked out, and he heard the bed creak as she jumped into it. How he wished he could find the words to ask her why she felt so happy. Being a Christian had become hard work for him. Eric also wondered what she did at the cottage next door with that blind girl. Susan always came home with her face fairly glowing after "seeing for Lisa."

Eric climbed into bed. He tried to think about all the questions life had been tossing his way, but before he knew what happened, sleep captured him.

The next two weeks passed quickly. Susan and Eric worked in Dr. Foster's office. Eric even had a chance to help when a weeping lady brought in her small white poodle. A car had crushed its tiny foot.

When they arrived home, Susan noticed that Eric looked for excuses to visit the storage shed. She knew that the chest in the shed contained some letters, a package of large pictures of the sea, a small locked wooden box, and some books. Why did he spend so much time there? Even Aunt Myrtle seemed to notice, but she said nothing.

"Aunt Myrtle," Susan said one evening when the sun had already plunged itself into the sea, "where is Eric?"

"He's out sitting on the sand staring at an empty page in his notebook."

Susan followed her gaze to the living room window. Eric sat just beyond the reach of the water. She could see his blond hair waving in the wind. "He's thinking again. I guess I better not bother him."

"I think you're right, Susan," Aunt Myrtle said. "Eric .as a lot on his mind these days. I wonder if he understood the discussion at the last baptismal class? Didn't you go over the 2,300-day prophecy in Daniel 8 and 9?"

"Yes. Dr. Foster said it's important to understand this and be able to explain it. It's easier to believe God when we see that He has a plan and that parts of that plan have already come true. I think it's exciting. Can I write it out for you? I need to practice explaining it to someone before class next week."

Aunt Myrtle opened her Bible to Daniel 8 and 9. She gave Susan a piece of paper and a pencil. Susan hesitated. "Just remember the five pillars," Aunt Myrtle suggested.

Susan made five spots on the paper and wrote down five dates. She wrote down the time represented by the distance between the spots. It looked like this:

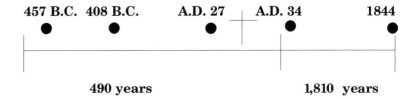

457 B.C.	408 B.C.	A.D. 27	A.D. 34	1844
●	●	●	●	●

490 years   1,810 years

"Now, can you explain these events and tell me why they are so important to you right now?" Aunt Myrtle asked.

"First, you have to know that a day stands for a year in prophecy," Susan explained. "Spot number one begins with the year 457 B.C. That's when King Artaxerxes said the Jews could return and rebuild their city, Jerusalem. By 408 B.C. the work was finished. The third pillar stands for A.D. 27 when Jesus was baptized. And in A.D. 34 Stephen was stoned. Between these two pillars, 3 and 4, Jesus died. His work was cut short in the middle of this week of prophecy."

Susan drew a deep breath and continued. "Pillar number 5 is marked 1844. That is the time Daniel said that God would begin to judge His people."

"Now you've told me the dates given by the prophet and the events they stand for, but what does it all mean?"

Susan shut her eyes, thinking hard. "God gave the Jewish people seventy weeks, or 490 years, between pillars 1 and 4, to share the good news of God's love with the world. After the Jews stoned Stephen for preaching about Jesus, God gave the special work of the Jews to others. He wanted all people to know He loved them."

"How many years would pass between the time that the gospel story should go to the world and the time of the judgment in 1844?" Aunt Myrtle probed.

Susan's lips moved as she figured in her head. "That's 1,810 years!" Susan said triumphantly. "Dr. Foster said the Bible tells us about many things that happened after 1844 and are yet to happen before Jesus comes again. I can't believe that God says so much about the future."

Aunt Myrtle studied Susan's face. "Why do you think it is so important to understand a prophecy, Susan?"

"Because it helps me trust Him. What God says, happens!"

"The best thing is that right now Jesus is our High Priest in the heavenly temple. He receives our prayers and is covering our sins with His own blood. He is our best Friend."

"Dr. Foster promised to explain the judgment and—"

"Susan! Aunt Myrtle! Come quick!" Eric shouted,

113

bursting into the room, eyes wide with amazement. "There are fish all over the place. Thousands of them. Come on!"

Susan's skin prickled. She didn't know if she wanted to see thousands of fish all over the place, but she followed Eric and Aunt Myrtle to the beach.

"What's happening?" Eric asked excitedly. "Where did they all come from and why?" He whirled about, waving his hands at the small silver fish that wiggled and flipped on the sand.

"Wonderful!" Aunt Myrtle exclaimed. "I was afraid you had missed this. These are grunions."

Susan stood still. She felt chills go up and down her skin. When she tried to reach out and touch a writhing fish, it flipped itself into the water and disappeared. Susan jumped.

"Oh!" she screeched when her bare foot landed on a thin, slippery body.

Eric captured several grunions, then let them flop into the water. Aunt Myrtle just stood and laughed at the twins. Then the tide moved shoreward and the fish flipped themselves into the water. Soon the beach lay still and empty except for three shadowy figures.

"These grunions come up with the highest tide from March to July. Females lay their eggs beneath the sand, and the male grunions fertilize the eggs. Then they return to the water," Aunt Myrtle explained.

"But if the tide is going out farther and farther, how will the baby fish get to the water when they hatch?" Eric asked when he found his voice.

"God has timed it just right, Eric. The tide won't come this far up the beach again until the eggs are ready to hatch. Then at just the right moment, the high tide will return and wash out the eggs. They actually hatch just as the water touches them. Another wave will carry the infant fish safely away to the sea."

"Perfect timing," Eric said softly. He shook his head. "So God *does* have plans and patterns, just like Daniel tells us. Maybe He has plans for me too."

19

The Escape!

I'm sorry. I thought I'd have this article done sooner," Aunt Myrtle apologized, looking at the twins' dreary faces. They gazed at the two bulging beach bags sitting near the kitchen door.

"But Aunt Myrtle," Eric groaned, "Kevin and Margo will be here any minute with the food. Can't you finish that thing later?"

"Look, the day is perfect!" Susan opened the door, and a stream of morning sunshine danced into the room and whirled around them.

At that moment a white Mercedes pulled into the driveway, and two doors flew open. Margo and Kevin jumped out lugging a picnic basket and two yellow beach bags. Margo waved goodbye to the man behind the wheel. He shouted something out the window, gunned the engine, and sped away in a cloud of dust.

"My dad's really something," Margo told the twins and Aunt Myrtle when she and Kevin arrived at the kitchen door. "He's got some meeting to go to today. I bet I don't see him until late tonight." For just an instant a sadness filled her eyes; then her usual smile chased it away.

"Aunt Myrtle—" Eric started.

Aunt Myrtle walked briskly to the door. "Why don't you four run along and get things set up on the lawn?

Throw some frisbees and take a dip. I'll be finished here in an hour, and I'll join you."

"We'll meet you at the big palm tree," Eric shouted as the four excited young people scampered down the steps and onto the warm sand lugging their gear.

"It's a good thing this spot isn't far from the house," Kevin teased. He put the bags and picnic basket down and dropped onto the grass beside them.

"If it weren't for you guys' giant appetites," Susan retorted, "we wouldn't need to bring the whole refrigerator with us." She grinned at Eric and Kevin.

"A point well spoken," Kevin conceded. "Hey, let's get wet!"

They all raced to the sand and into the cool water, screaming and jumping about in the frothy waves.

"I'm hungry," Kevin announced when they'd returned to the picnic area.

"We aren't eating until Aunt Myrtle gets here," Susan said firmly.

"Aw, come on. Just a tiny crumb," Kevin begged.

"Don't you guys ever do anything without your aunt?" Margo asked. "I can go anywhere I please. No one at my house ever asks me what I'm doing. Dad just says, 'Behave yourself.' "

Before Eric could think how to explain that he enjoyed going with Aunt Myrtle without sounding like a dependent little kid, Kevin reached over and yanked Margo's wet hair.

"Bet you wished your mom and dad had some time to tag along with you, huh, Margo." He got up and started to unload the picnic basket. "Just getting things arranged," he explained quickly when he saw Susan glaring at him, then wandered off to explore a nearby path.

Eric got out his sketch pad, and Susan and Margo

stretched out on their towels.

"Hey, Margo, what goes?"

Eric looked up to see a tall, dark-haired boy grinning at them. Water dripped from two broad, tanned shoulders onto a red surfboard he held under one arm. Beside him stood a shorter boy who also carried a sleek board. He sized up Eric with a frown.

"Oh, hi, Jerry . . . and Fred. These are some new friends from the East Coast," Margo introduced the twins.

Eric stared at the guy called Jerry, who looked massive. Fred walked over to Eric and peered over his shoulder.

"So you're an artist. My old man dabs at that stuff. Kind of tweaky, I'd say."

"Knock it off," Jerry said, glaring at Fred. "Hey, there's a great party going on down at the beach," he said to Margo. "Bring your friends along. We have booze and great sounds." He snapped the fingers on one hand and patted Margo's cheek with the other. "It'll be a bore without you, babe."

Eric felt so mad he was afraid Jerry would notice his clenched fists and red face. The worst thing was that Margo looked as though she wished she could go.

"Say, Jerry," Susan said, "we're having a picnic here right now, and . . . I don't think we want to—"

"We could go for an hour," Margo suggested. "Aunt Myrtle won't be along for a while."

Kevin walked up and gave Jerry a punch on one of his massive shoulders.

Eric gulped. Jerry grinned and jabbed Kevin back. Eric watched the boys exchange a series of mock punches that seemed to say they had been good friends once, but a wary distance now existed, even though no one mentioned it in words.

"I haven't see you around," Kevin said.

"I'm working for my old man this summer," Jerry said.

"Susan, Eric! Just wait until you see!" Everyone looked up to see Aunt Myrtle arrive at the picnic table. "Hi, Jerry and Fred. It's good to see you." Aunt Myrtle put her bag down on the grass and smiled at the boys.

"Hey, man, I gotta get going," Fred mumbled. "Jerry—"

"There's enough food here to turn us into blimps." Aunt Myrtle laughed. "Why don't you join us?"

"We'd like that," Kevin added, taking Jerry's arm and leading him to the table.

"What about the gang and—" Fred's voice trailed off.

"I guess it can wait. This lady is a great cook." Jerry winked at Aunt Myrtle. They all laughed except Fred, who excused himself and walked away.

Eric and Susan exchanged questioning glances.

"So what were you so excited about a minute ago?" Kevin questioned Aunt Myrtle before they could begin to dish up the food.

"I'll just show you," she said, leading them off the grass and down the beach toward the rocks. "I saw a fantastic giant green sea anemone right here somewhere." She glanced about the tide pools. "Look at this!" She stooped down, and the others crowded around the pool. There beneath the water a flowerlike green object with dozens of thin, round tentacles clutched a rock. The tentacles waved back and forth in the ebb and flow of water.

"It's beautiful," Margo breathed. "I've never seen one so large."

"Watch this," Aunt Myrtle said. She dropped an open mussel shell into the sea anemone. Instantly, the tentacles pulled together toward the center and grasped the shell and drew it into its center. Moments later the sea anemone shoved the empty shell out into the pool. It expanded its tentacles, allowing them to undulate in the water.

Kevin's eyes widened. "That thing looks so innocent."

"It only seems that way, Kevin. Along the edges of those soft tentacles are stinging cells of poison that paralyze any prey that is swept past by a surge of water."

"But it looks like a harmless plant!" Jerry frowned at Aunt Myrtle.

"Don't believe it!" Aunt Myrtle laughed. "This animal means business. Entrapment is its game."

"Sort of reminds me of Satan," Susan blurted. "He always tries to get me to do things that he knows God doesn't want me to do. He really makes them look good too."

Eric wanted to look at Jerry and Margo, but he kept his eyes on the tide pool. But he wondered what they were thinking. Suddenly Jerry reached down and poked his finger into the sea anemone. They all watched the tentacles tighten around his finger.

"You are a bit too large for his dinner." Aunt Myrtle laughed.

"Imagine a fish swimming along. He sees those swaying arms inviting him to find a safe shelter there; then *swoosh*, he's instantly sucked into a trap. Man, he's in big trouble," Jerry said. "He's just being dissolved away. He's had it!"

Aunt Myrtle smiled. "Thank God we aren't a helpless victim in a tide pool. We can still choose to avoid the traps that Satan sets. We can recognize them for what they are, thanks to the Holy Spirit. God doesn't go away and leave us when we're caught in the tentacles of sin. It hurts Him, but He just keeps on loving us."

"I'm sure glad I finally got to know Him," Susan sighed. "But it's still hard to know just what to choose to do and where to go. You have to choose what to wear and lots of other things."

"There are some guides that my dad gave me," Kevin said. "They've helped me more than once to decide what to do."

"What guides?" Jerry asked, sitting down on a rock.

"The first guide is Will this make me want to know God better? I think that's what Satan fears most. The second guide is to think about having Jesus along. I mean, would He join me in what I'm doing?" Kevin looked at the sea anemone's waving tentacles. "No matter how good it looks," he added.

"What's the third guide?" Jerry asked.

"I should consider carefully whether this choice will make me healthier and bring lasting joy to myself and others."

Everyone looked at each other and smiled. Jerry gave Kevin a punch on the arm, then rose to leave. "I'd like to see you around again sometime, Kevin. Thanks, Aunt Myrtle. Guess I'll be getting home now. Something tells me there are a few tentacles I need to escape."

"You aren't the only one who's thinking that," Eric mumbled. He glanced around at the others.

They nodded silently. Aunt Myrtle didn't say a word. She just started back to the picnic table.

20

The Law of Life

I don't see why Dr. Foster has to have our class out here on these awful rocks," Margo grumbled to Susan as they picked their way down the rough cliff toward the sea.

"I don't either," Susan said, "but I like the idea."

"Everyone get yourselves settled around this large pool," Dr. Foster commanded. He reached into his pack and pulled out five small Bibles. Everyone took one.

"I've brought you here for a reason," Dr. Foster began.

"Sure. Sunburn and limp hair," Margo complained in a whisper.

Susan cast Eric a glance. Even he seemed disgusted by Margo's grumbling.

"What do you see happening here?" Dr. Foster asked, ignoring Margo's complaint. "Look around you."

"The sea is coming in and going out," Kevin observed.

"Right," Dr. Foster said, "but what is accomplished when it flows in and out of a pool?"

Everyone leaned over the pool and watched the edge of a wave send fresh water up the ravine in the rocks and saw it surge into the pool before it flowed back to the sea.

"Food must come in to feed sea anemones and fish," Susan suggested.

"Keep looking around you," Dr. Foster ordered. "What else is happening?"

"Pelicans!" Eric shouted, pointing to three large forms that cruised just above the sea. One suddenly dropped like a bomb into the surf. His body and wings seemed to splatter over the surface while his great bill plunged into the water. In an instant he gathered his strewn parts together and lifted a bulging bill from the water, threw his head back, and gulped down its contents.

"OK, pelicans eat the fish." Dr. Foster laughed.

"I know!" Margo brightened. "The mists rise up from the sea and later fall as rain that will return to the sea by the rivers and streams."

"Good!" Dr. Foster encouraged. "Anything else?"

"I see an empty mussel shell. I suppose a starfish did that," Susan said.

"And the broken shells grind up in the pools and finally become sand," Kevin added. He reached into the pool and grabbed a handful of fine sand and let it run through his fingers back into the pool.

"Some creatures hide in the sand and send up long siphons to the surface to strain minute life from the incoming seawater," Dr. Foster said. "Do you see a pattern in all this?"

"I think . . . Does it mean . . . everything receives from something else?" Susan questioned.

"Yes, Susan, but what else?"

"When it gets something, it also ends up giving to some other form of life," Kevin observed.

"Now you have it!" Dr. Foster flashed them a grin that made the whole world brighter.

"Giving and receiving. That's nature. Nothing lives to itself," Dr. Foster continued. "Now what do you think would happen if any form of life just stayed to itself and never gave to the good of the community?"

Everyone stared into the pool. They tried to imagine what it would be like if the sea quit bringing in fresh water and the discarded shells didn't become sand and there were no more fish that hid in the shelter of the seaweed.

"Giving is the law of life," Dr. Foster said. "God is the great source of everything. He sent Jesus to us to help us know Himself and to save us. We receive His love and, in turn, reach out to help others. We return praise to God for His love and so do others. This completes a circle of love and service. God doesn't want that circle to be broken." Dr. Foster drew a circle in a sandy crevice between two rocks.

"Hey, that's like an electrical circuit," Kevin explained. "It has to be completed before you get light. Anything that interrupts the circuit keeps the light from coming on. That's the law of electricity."

"Good illustration." Dr. Foster smiled. "Now what else do you think we have that we need to share with others and with God?"

"I suppose our money," Margo groaned.

"Actually, God asks for one-tenth of our money and one-seventh of our time. Leviticus 27:32 says one-tenth belongs to the Lord, and the command to give one day in seven, the seventh day to be exact, is found in Exodus 20." Eric grinned triumphantly.

Everyone stared at Eric. He suddenly turned red and looked down into the pool. Susan wondered just how he knew the answer and the text. She didn't think anyone had explained tithing to Eric.

"Wow!" Margo breathed. "That's $1 out of every $10. I'll never get anything saved if I do that!"

Everyone laughed at Margo except Dr. Foster. "Actually, Margo has brought up a good point. Will paying

God the tithe and also giving offerings to help support His work make us poorer?"

"Of course it will," Eric said emphatically. "I can add. If you give money away, it's gone. Of course, we should still share some and obey God about the tithe."

"I think it's time for a promise," Dr. Foster said. "Open your Bibles to Luke 6:38. Kevin, will you read that to us?"

Kevin cleared his throat, then read, " 'Give, and it will be given to you; good measure, pressed down, shaken together, running over, will be put into your lap. For the measure you give will be the measure you get back' " (RSV).

"That doesn't sound like poverty to me," Susan said. "I think if we obey God and give our time and our money in the way He has asked us to, we will be very happy and have all we need."

"Exactly," Dr. Foster responded. "If we don't, we will become like a tide pool that the sea no longer refills. We will be selfish and stagnant. No life can exist very long in that condition."

"Are you trying to say that it is for our own good that God asks us to keep His Sabbath and return the tithe to Him?" Margo asked.

"When you think of it, everything belongs to Him in the first place. I guess we're just managers of His possessions. So it must be best for us to give as well as to receive," Kevin answered for Dr. Foster.

"Wow, it's later than I realized," Dr. Foster said, closing his Bible. "We'd better scoot. Aunt Myrtle will wonder if you've all been washed out to sea."

They climbed the cliff to the path and started toward the house. Dr. Foster took Kevin and Margo home in his Jeep, leaving the twins to walk home alone.

"Boy, this business of being a Christian is getting so

complicated," Eric groaned. "Now it's money too."

"Oh, isn't it wonderful, Eric. God lets us be His partners!"

There she goes being glad again, Eric thought to himself. They entered the house and found a note on the kitchen table saying Aunt Myrtle was out.

"Eric," Susan said, planting both hands on her hips and staring into his face. "You tell me how you knew those texts today. No one has ever explained this stuff to you before."

"OK, I will, or I'll never get any peace. I found a book in Aunt Myrtle's chest. Look! It has verses about everything you can ever imagine."

Susan ran her finger over the title. *"Bible Readings for the Home,"* she read. Just then a picture dropped from the book. Eric scrambled to pick it up, but Susan had already seen it. "What's that?" she demanded.

"I don't know. Just an old photo I found."

Susan grabbed the picture. The smiling face of a tall, very skinny boy looked up at her. At the bottom of the picture she saw the words *Your Sailor Boy*.

"Let's go borrow Aunt Myrtle's magnifying glass. Maybe we can tell who it is. It has to be someone we know."

Eric didn't argue. They ran to Aunt Myrtle's study and started to search her desktop. There stood a picture of the same smiling boy.

"Wow!" Eric whistled softly. "What a find."

"Turn it over," Susan urged. "See what it says on the back."

"Well! What have we here?" Aunt Myrtle's voice filled the whole room.

Eric and Susan whirled around to face a pair of very stern eyes.

21

Valuable Gifts

A great silence engulfed Eric and Susan. It screamed at them. Eric wanted to crawl under the carpet and never come out. He glanced at Susan. She looked like a naughty puppy caught in the act of chewing up someone's slipper. Her eyes shone with tears about to spill over, and they got bigger every second.

They both just stood there with clammy hands, clinging to the two worn photographs. Aunt Myrtle stared at Eric, then at Susan. The seconds became mountains of time filled with a wilderness of thoughts. Eric feared it would swallow him up. He wanted to say something, but the words caught in his dry throat. Regret stabbed at his insides. *Why didn't Aunt Myrtle just yell at them and have it done with? She trusted us and now—Oh, how dumb could I be?* Eric thought in despair.

Suddenly Aunt Myrtle's eyes softened. She sighed and slumped into a chair near the window.

"Aunt Myrtle, we didn't mean to—we just wanted to— We—" Eric stammered.

Susan stared at Eric. This couldn't be the same Eric who always acted so cool, as though nothing mattered.

"I haven't meant to be such a mystery person," Aunt Myrtle began. She motioned for the twins to come to her.

They flopped onto the carpet near her chair.

"You see, it's rather hard to explain things to someone else when you aren't sure just what it all means to yourself yet," she went on.

"Boy, I understand that." Eric nodded. "A lot of things confuse me these days." He edged closer and patted Aunt Myrtle's arm in an awkward way.

Susan flung herself into Aunt Myrtle's arms. "I'm sorry," she sobbed. "It's all my fault we snooped. You won't be angry, will you? I love you, Aunt Myrtle."

Eric sighed. He wished he could express his feelings so easily. *I am doing better, though,* he thought. *Knowing Jesus has made it easier.*

"You two knobby heads." Aunt Myrtle smiled, using Dr. Foster's name for them. "You've been doing some detective work in the storage shed! Eric, just keep the book. It answered a lot of questions for me when I was your age."

Eric's mouth flew open. Susan thought an eagle could have nested inside it. "I only scanned a couple of your letters, honest, that's all," Eric stumbled through the words.

"I know, and I forgive you both," Aunt Myrtle said. A smile formed around her mouth and eyes. "How about an agreement?" she asked. "We will agree to talk with each other, especially whenever we are about to be overcome with curiosity that could hurt one of us. And also when we really need answers."

"I agree!" Eric shouted. "And I'm sorry," he added.

Susan agreed with her eyes. All the heaviness just lifted like a fluffy cloud and sailed away with Aunt Myrtle's smile.

"Now I'm not going to be able to solve all the mystery for you because it hasn't been solved for me yet. You see,

I'm curious just like you are."

"But who is Sailor Boy?" Susan blurted.

"Susan!" Eric growled, jabbing her with his elbow.

"It's all right, Eric. Susan, that's part of the mystery I think best left for later. I'll tell you a little about my life, though. I met Sailor Boy over twelve years ago, and, of course, I fell in love with him. We planned to marry and spend every evening dreaming in that observation room of yours, Eric. He loved the sea, just as I do."

"But why did you send him away and—" Susan interrupted.

"I didn't, Susan. He, as well as my other friends, went off to college while I decided to wait a year so that I could care for my sick mother. Sailor Boy met a girl at school who captured his heart. I just never stopped loving him, I guess."

"Why do you have his picture around after all these years?" Eric asked, trying not to be too curious.

"Because, well, we've been friends over the years. I—"

"It's none of our business!" Susan scolded. "Eric, when Aunt Myrtle is ready, she will tell us."

Aunt Myrtle threw back her head and laughed. The tension melted away.

"Children," she started again. "Let me tell you that I am considering marrying this Sailor Boy. He is no longer married. His wife is dead. He has asked me to be his wife. Perhaps you would join me in praying about it. You see, I want to use my gifts for God, and I must be sure marriage would allow for that. I love God very much."

"We will, Aunt Myrtle, we will," the twins agreed, looking at each other with serious eyes.

"But what do you mean about your gifts?" Susan asked.

"Miss Question Box, come with me, and I will show

129

you. Eric, you're welcome to join us."

Eric and Susan followed Aunt Myrtle to the beach. Eric felt happy to know Aunt Myrtle might be able to have a dream come true. He had dreams too. But what would happen to them? Eric liked the big house by the sea. He hadn't realized until just this minute just how much he wanted to stay right here in this house with his aunt and Susan. But what about Dad? His letters were so few now, and he seemed so busy with his own life. He still hadn't said when he could move to California and they would be together again. Eric felt confused.

"What do you think is one of the most valuable things on this beach?" Aunt Myrtle asked.

The twins scanned the water and the sand. They looked at the rocks that cupped small tide pools and gazed at the blue sky overhead filled with saucy gulls.

"It all has to be valuable," Eric objected. "How can anyone say what is most important?"

"Right! But tell me this. If you could vote for what seemed least valuable or exciting about this place, what would it be?"

"The sand!" Susan shouted. "It gets into sandwiches and our eyes. Of course, some creatures hide in it, so that's important."

"Yeah," Eric agreed. "Sand isn't exciting like the seals and whales and shells are."

"Have you ever heard of silicone?" Aunt Myrtle asked.

"Sure," Eric said. "It's used in waterproofing things and—sand! You mean that sand is—Of course it is! Sand it superimportant."

"Glass! Sand is used in making glass!" Susan cried. "Think of microscopes and telescopes and lenses for cameras." She scooped up a handful of precious sand and let it sift through her fingers.

"People are like sand. They seem useless sometimes, even irritating. God sees what they can become, just like some scientist saw sand as valuable. He gives each one of us special gifts. They are called spiritual gifts because God gives them through the Holy Spirit."

"When do people get these gifts?" Eric asked, trying not to appear too anxious.

"When we accept Him as our friend and are baptized," Aunt Myrtle explained. "We receive the Holy Spirit in a special way. We become part of God's church body and receive abilities that help support God's work and family. These gifts will also make us happy."

Eric could hardly believe his ears. God would give him his own unique way to serve! Perhaps someday his confusion about his future would be gone. He realized that he needed to know God better and listen to His words. "You mean I don't have to be like someone else?" he asked cautiously.

"Dad wants Eric to be a lawyer like him," Susan explained. "Eric would hate that. He likes to be quiet and read. He doesn't like lots of people and noise and stuff."

Aunt Myrtle tousled Eric's shock of blond hair and laughed. Then she looked at him in her serious way. "God has made you special, Eric. He has a plan for your life. You must ask Him to show it to you. He knows the key that will unlock your heart. Just trust Him."

"I just hate to feel confused," Eric mumbled.

"Eric, I'll tell you about the Holy Spirit and how to stay close to Jesus. Then you won't be confused. Aunt Myrtle explained it to me when you were off camping with Kevin," Susan said earnestly.

Eric reached out and gave Susan's ponytail a flip. They all laughed.

"Aunt Myrtle," Susan said as they climbed the steps to

the house. "Don't worry about Sailor Boy. Whoever he is, God will work things out." Susan laughed and went into the house singing. She just couldn't help it.

22

The Intruder

The fifty-foot yacht *Sunfish* cut through the gentle swells that rippled across the bay. Cool, salty spray shot up onto the twins as they huddled in the bow. They peered into the thin mists that whispered through the channel between the mainland and Anacapa Island.

"Susan, listen!" Eric commanded.

Susan stopped trailing her finger through the walls of green waves that played beside the ship and closed her eyes tight in concentration.

"Over there!" Eric shouted above the motors.

Suddenly a tiny flash of light reached them, and a low groaning noise tumbled over the water and landed in the bow of the ship with them.

"It's a lighthouse, and that's the foghorn bellowing," Aunt Myrtle shouted. She handed her field glasses to Susan.

Susan tried to focus on the dark jut of land that hid in the misty morning. She could just make out the form of a lighthouse perched at one end of a rocky point of land. It flashed its beam at them and disappeared into the fog.

"Sounds like a hoarse old bullfrog!" Eric laughed.

Susan doubled over with laughter and almost slipped on the wet deck. She grabbed at the guardrail and steadied herself as the ship rose up and over a large swell, landing at the bottom of it with a bang.

The anticipation of reaching the island churned inside Susan until she could hardly stop jumping about. *What kind of special discoveries awaited her?* she wondered. Then suddenly they had arrived. She made her way up the long, steep steps of a ladder from the ship to the dock built on a great rock high above the water.

"Well, that wasn't so bad," Aunt Myrtle sighed as she reached the top of the stairway that clung to the cliff's face. She swirled around, taking in the view of the tiny island in one glance. Western gulls swooped and squawked above nests that snuggled in the dry grass at the island's edge.

The twins followed Aunt Myrtle as she showed them the way to a trail. Soon they arrived at a flat spot high above the sea. Aunt Myrtle stopped and placed her hands on her hips. She scowled down at some plants that carpeted the entire area. Susan and Eric exchanged puzzled glances.

"One of these days when I come out here there will be nothing but ice plant," she moaned. "It just takes over."

"But it's pretty," Susan objected. "There are yellow blooms in the spring and—"

"Let me tell you something about this stuff," Aunt Myrtle interrupted. "Somehow it arrived here. I don't know if seeds or bits of the plant rafted over on driftwood or stuck in a bird's wing or what, but it doesn't belong on the island."

Eric looked around. He still felt puzzled.

"You see, the ecosystems on this island are very fragile. Any plant or animal that intrudes can upset the balance and even cause other forms of life to disappear."

Susan stooped down and touched the thick tubelike

plant. Its stalks were covered with tiny droplets of water. When she broke open a small stem, it oozed fluid.

"Wow, and it's so dry over here!" she exclaimed.

"That's just it. This plant is able to absorb moisture from the air itself," Aunt Myrtle explained.

"Why doesn't the growth of other plants keep it in check?" Eric asked, remembering his botany class. "Aren't most places able to support many plants?"

"These plants absorb so much salt with the water they take in that it leaches into the surrounding soil. Not many other plants can tolerate that much salt. So they just die off, leaving room for more ice plant. Santa Barbara Island near here is almost overtaken with it. It may seem nice, but when it forms a thick mat over the island, all the true plants meant to live here will just be gone."

"It reminds me of Satan," Susan blurted. She gazed at a mass of blubbery seals' bodies on a sandy spit of land beneath them. "God made everything so perfect. Then Satan messed it all up. Maybe if this island gets messed up, the seals won't come back anymore."

"Is that the way it is with God's special Sabbath day?" Eric thought out loud. "I really look forward to it every week. There are so many great ways to learn to know more about God. No wonder God gave us the Sabbath." Eric looked at Aunt Myrtle and suddenly felt shy.

"You're right! Satan does try to counterfeit every good thing God has given us. He made a false Sabbath and planned that men would soon forget the seventh-day Sabbath of God's commandments. Worshiping on the false Sabbath seems to be taking over our world like this crystalline ice plant is taking over the island."

"I know the Sabbath is important," Susan said, remembering the class time spent looking up Bible texts.

"But, well, is it really all that important?"

"If God says to do something, Susan, how can you argue with that?" Eric said.

"The Sabbath is like a seal," Aunt Myrtle explained. "Not that kind of seal," she laughed, noticing that Susan stared at the forms far below on the beach.

"You mean a seal of a country that shows the name, title, and territory of that country?" Eric questioned.

"You've been studying by yourself again," Susan groaned. "You promised to study with me."

"I will," Eric said. "It's just that I can't stop reading sometimes. There are a million things I need to learn. I want to be sure I know everything I need to about getting to heaven. Man, I wouldn't want to miss heaven just because I did something wrong. I even have a list—" He stopped when he saw the frown on Aunt Myrtle's face.

"Tell us how Sabbath is like a seal of God," Susan reminded.

Aunt Myrtle seemed not to hear her and gazed at Eric for a long time. Eric thought she looked a bit worried. He wondered if she knew how hard he was trying to obey God and be good and just how miserable he felt because he didn't seem to be able to do everything right. He felt like the ice plant of fear and anger was about to take over his inner island of joy. Being a Christian was just plain tougher than he'd imagined. Still . . .

Finally, Aunt Myrtle spoke. "When we obey God and love His Sabbath as He wants us to, we show that we choose Him, and He seals us to Himself much the way a president stamps his seal upon something he has agreed upon or accepted. The Sabbath has His name, Lord. It has His title, Creator and God. It also contains the territory over which He is king, the heavens and the earth. Exodus 20:8-11 tells us that."

"When we keep the Sabbath, we show our loyalty to God," Eric added. "I want to be loyal to God."

"I'm glad to hear you say that, Eric. There have always been those who have obeyed God's law and loved Him—all through earth's history." Aunt Myrtle smiled.

"Sabbath is a celebration of God's creation," Susan added. "So how can anyone make a Sabbath?"

"Of course they can't, Susan. But God knew that Satan would use men like the evil Emperor Constantine and religious groups who thought they could be like God and change His holy law. Many times people just don't think about what they are doing when they allow practices to take over their lives. Like this ice plant, error takes over and truth is crowded out. The seventh day has always been God's Sabbath, and those who love Him obey it. The disciples kept His day, and we enjoy it today."

"I wish Jesus would come so everything would be back to the happy time Adam and Eve had in their garden home," Susan sighed. "I can't wait to see Him."

Aunt Myrtle nodded in agreement. A gull drifted past on an unseen wind current. The sea splashed against the rocks below. Eric felt that heaven must be a terrific place. He wanted to go there. He felt determined to obey God. Still, it worried him. What if he couldn't be good enough?

"By the way," Aunt Myrtle began, looking suddenly shy. "I have decided to accept Sailor Boy's proposal."

Aunt Myrtle's dream is coming true! Eric thought.

"Oh, Aunt Myrtle, how wonderful!" Susan's eyes danced.

"Aren't you even going to ask who this mystery man is?" Aunt Myrtle teased.

The twins held their breath, but their eyes pleaded

with Aunt Myrtle for an answer.

"He has another name, you know," Aunt Myrtle continued. "His name is Frank," she said in a soft voice. "His name is Frank."

23

Eric's Cry for Help

Aunt Myrtle's words rose up into the mist that hovered in thin fingers over Anacapa Island. She smiled at the twins, who were staring at each other in stunned silence.

"Frank!" Susan finally shouted, coming to life. "That's our dad!" She danced about on the dusty path that wiggled its way across the tiny island. "Oh, that's so wonderful!"

Eric sat down beside the trail. He grinned at Aunt Myrtle. A feeling of warmth flooded through him, but he couldn't find any words to say. He watched Susan flinging her arms about and letting her joy fly up like sea gulls and soar out over the glistening sea.

"Together! We'll all live together in the house by the sea," she shouted.

Eric laughed to himself. Aunt Myrtle would make sure they saw beautiful things together. Then all the anger inside Dad would melt away. Maybe his own confusion would just evaporate like the mists over Anacapa when the sun beamed through.

Just then a western gull squawked at him from her nest near the edge of the cliff. She stretched her black wings and climbed off the grassy nest, turning her head so that he could see the bright red spot on her orange bill. Then she sailed away on an unseen air current.

"Wow! What a view," Eric breathed softly to no one in particular. "I'm going to get a shot of those three eggs."

He flopped onto his stomach and inched his way toward the hollowed-out place in the grass. Soon he could see that one egg had already hatched. A small, spotted, wet gull huddled beside pieces of broken shell.

Eric focused his camera, then decided to move just a bit closer. Perhaps another shell would crack open.

Suddenly six brown pelicans glided around the corner of the island toward Eric. They flew in ragged formation just above him. He could see the details of the feathers in their outstretched wings. Eric flung himself onto his back and started to focus his camera on their brown bellies. But before he could press the shutter, he felt his body begin to slide on the loose rocks. Instantly he realized his mistake in moving too close to the cliff's edge.

Terror raced through his body like stampeding elephants. His hands reached out and found only dry grass. He dug his heels into the gravel. Only one word escaped from his dry throat. "Help!"

All in a second, his head protruded over nothingness. He could hear the surf smashing against sharp rocks 200 feet below him. A gull swooped over his face, screaming at him. Fear plunged its giant fist into his stomach. He wasn't ready to die. How could God save him? He remembered the list of good things he'd meant to do hidden in the book beneath his bed at home.

Then two hands grasped his ankles and held on. He felt his body stop with a jerk as the hands drew him slowly back from the cliff's edge and certain death.

He looked up into the stern eyes of a camp ranger as Aunt Myrtle and Susan flung their arms around him and sobbed out their relief.

For two hours Eric sat in the cabin of the yacht as it

sailed away from the island. The fist of fear began to open, yet it didn't completely leave him.

"Oh, Eric!" Susan said for the tenth time. She'd refused to move an inch from his side. Her eyes spoke the words none of them could say aloud: What if Eric had died, just like Mother? Eric felt angry with himself for his carelessness.

"Aunt Myrtle," Susan whispered, "I wish Jesus would come."

Aunt Myrtle sighed. "I do too, Susan. There is a promise in John 14:3 that I always remember when my heart is lonely to see Him. Jesus promises us that He has gone to prepare beautiful homes for us and that He is coming back to take us home to live with Him."

"How will we know where to find Him, and how will we know who He is?" Susan asked. She frowned and looked up into Aunt Myrtle's face.

"Oh, Susan, you won't have any trouble knowing Him! Unlike anyone else who claims to be Christ, Jesus will come in the clouds, and thousands of glorious angels will be with Him. He won't walk with us on this earth; He will catch us up into the sky to meet Him there."

"But what about—I mean, the dead people, will they—?"

Aunt Myrtle hugged Susan close. She smiled at Eric, who huddled against the cabin window watching the waves spew up. "Those who have died and who have loved Him will be given new life. And they will rise into the air to meet Jesus too. Can't you just imagine that?"

Susan pressed her face against the window and scanned the blue sky. Happy faces danced across the screen of her mind. Just think, she would see Mother again. It made joy bubble up inside her. She turned and smiled at Aunt Myrtle and Eric.

Eric tried to smile at Susan, but inside he didn't feel the joy Susan did. He felt that old knot of fear twisting in his stomach. There would be lots of trouble before Jesus came again. Wars and hate would fill the earth. Matthew 24 said so. People would pretend to be Jesus. The worst thing was that he didn't see how he could get ready. How could Jesus ever take him to heaven when he still did so many bad things?

Eric watched Susan as she studied the sky through the cabin window. Why did she feel so happy and content with Aunt Myrtle's simple explanation? It was as though Susan knew Jesus wouldn't forget them when He came. He wanted to ask her, but couldn't. Susan didn't claim to be perfect. It was a good thing because Eric knew she wasn't. Then why did she glow with anticipation at the idea of Jesus coming soon?

"Look!" Aunt Myrtle exclaimed, pointing toward the ghostly form of Anacapa. "I've seen the island in the early spring when the giant coreopsis blooms. That great yellow and red wildflower covers the island with a mass of color that can be seen from the mainland. When I see the golden glow, I know spring is near. And when we see the signs described in the Bible, we know Jesus is coming soon."

Eric determined to read Matthew 24 again for himself.

"These things are written to make us glad and not afraid," Aunt Myrtle said softly, looking at Eric.

All the way home Eric thought about the golden flower that welcomed spring, and how he knew Aunt Myrtle would rush down to the dock to get a ticket for a ride to Anacapa. Perhaps as she came closer and closer to that ragged place, the yellow-gold would rise up through the mists and welcome her. Could Jesus' coming be like that? Friends welcoming friends? Maybe for some good people, but what about him?

"A letter from Dad!" Susan screamed as she entered the kitchen after their long journey had ended at last.

The twins tore open the envelope and read:

Hi, kids!

I'm in a bit of a hurry, but I wanted you to know the good news. Aunt Myrtle and I plan to be married before school begins in the fall.

I would have told you sooner, but it took me some time to convince Myrtle that she belonged with us here in Maryland.

My law practice is developing rapidly, and I just can't leave here at this time. I'm sure you understand that.

Myrtle doesn't mean to take your mother's place. No one can do that. But I know we will all be happy together. Eric, please help in any way you can.

More details later.

Dad

Eric stared at the letter. He remembered fooling with the keys in the lock on the chest in Aunt Myrtle's storage shed. When he'd placed the right key into the lock, it had turned easily. Aunt Myrtle leaving the house by the sea? That idea just didn't fit. How would she ever be happy away from her castle by the sea? Why didn't Dad understand that? He glanced at Aunt Myrtle, who was studying a letter of her own. Her face held a stiff expression, as though she didn't want it to talk.

She paused and looked at the twins. "I guess he's told you, then? It means a very busy month for us, doesn't it?"

For the second time that day, Eric felt something rise up inside and cry *Help!*—this time for a reason he didn't understand.

"It'll be all right," Aunt Myrtle continued smoothly. She gave them a thin smile and walked out of the room.

24

A Robe for Eric

Judgment!" an unseen voice shouted. The music of a thousand silver trumpets filled the great hall. A golden throne sat in the center of the room surrounded by beings wearing soft, white garments. Behind the throne arched a rainbow that shimmered and reflected colors onto the marble walls.

Suddenly all the beings hushed their voices and folded their wings. A door opened and a great Presence, shining like the noonday sun, entered. He glided over the crystal floor and settled onto the throne. For one instant silence filled the room; then every voice cried out in joyous song, "Glory, glory to God in the highest heaven!"

Eric and Susan gazed up at the Being on the throne. His eyes flashed like lightning. The light nearly blinded Eric. He crouched and covered his face with his hands.

Eric heard the Being call out Susan's name. He watched as she hesitated. Then another Being with scars on His hands motioned for her to come to Him. Eric knew it must be Jesus. Susan ran gladly to Jesus, and together they walked toward the golden throne. Eric noticed for the first time that Susan wore a white garment that covered her entirely.

"Come, child," the great Being on the throne said.

"Father," Jesus said, "this is Susan, My friend."

Eric listened in amazement. The voice of Jesus filled the whole hall with sweetness, and at its sound the voices of every being lifted in songs of joy.

"Dear child," the voice of God continued, "I know you have sinned greatly, but Jesus has covered every sin with His blood." He opened a book and studied its pages. Eric saw that across every page were written the words, *Forgiven by My blood.* He could not read a single sin. He saw Susan's face shine with joy as she realized Jesus had covered them all.

"I see that you are wearing the robe my Son gave you," the voice continued. "There is great joy in My heart. I have long waited for this day. Welcome home!"

Then, as though nothing could ever have stopped them, every being in the great hall sang out, "Glory, glory to the Lamb who was slain!"

Jesus took Susan's hand and led her through a silver door. They disappeared from Eric's sight.

"Wait for me!" Eric screamed in terror. "Wait!" He turned toward the throne to plead. Every eye looked at him. Thoughts scrambled themselves together in his mind. *You've tried so hard. You're as good as Susan. What about the book under the bed with the list of good things you've done and all the bad things you didn't do? God will listen to that.* But then the thoughts fell like an empty glass and shattered on the floor. "My son," God's voice called out to him.

He had to go to the awful throne! His wobbly legs carried him there against his will. He wanted to hide.

"My son," God spoke again. His voice sounded full of a great sadness. "Who is here to speak for you? I have your record before Me."

Eric covered his face with his arms and peeked at the pages of his book. Every ugly deed and thought stared

145

back at him. No lovely word *Forgiven* covered them. He hadn't meant to do any of those things. He had wanted to obey God so much. He had wanted to believe. Why had he tried to be good all by himself? Why, why, why?

"I'm so sorry, son," God said sadly. "Jesus cannot come to defend you, because you never asked Him to. He wanted to very much. You wanted to control your own life and make your own choices."

Eric groaned. He glanced toward the silver door, and hope arose within him because Jesus stood there.

"Jesus, speak for me!" he cried.

Jesus bowed His head in His hands and wept. Every being in the hall wept with Him. He didn't come to Eric's aid.

Eric realized that He couldn't come because Eric had never asked Him to. Now it was too late. He heard great sobs fill the room and realized they were his.

"Son," God continued. "Where is the robe? Did no one give it to you, no one ever offer it to you?"

Suddenly Eric remembered the many times Susan and Aunt Myrtle had tried to talk with him about a robe. Susan said it was what she wore that made her happy and free, even though she was not good herself. He remembered how many times he had pushed the words away and gone on trying to be good by himself.

"Yes . . . I . . . but . . ." No excuse would come out. "I do not have the robe," he cried finally, looking down at his own garments that clearly showed stains and filth.

"I'm grieved, My son, but you cannot live here. You have chosen another way. You would not be happy here. Oh, My son!" Suddenly God turned His face away.

Sorrow and fear hurled themselves together and washed over Eric. A great blackness surrounded him, and he felt himself falling, falling, falling. "Help, please, help!" Eric screamed into a darkness.

"Eric! What's the matter? Wake up!" Susan cried, shaking him by the shoulders.

"Susan, it's you!" Eric's eyes opened wide as he stared at her surprised face.

"Of course it's me, silly! You've had a nightmare. Look at your bed! It's torn to pieces."

Susan started to laugh until she noticed Eric's face. Fear, relief, and tears jumbled together across his face. His body shook and shivered.

"Eric?" Aunt Myrtle entered the room and looked at him with questioning eyes. "Are you all right?"

"The judgment is coming," Eric sobbed. "It's wonderful and terrible."

"Yes," Aunt Myrtle agreed, "but what—"

"Oh, Aunt Myrtle, God was so sad! But He couldn't take me into heaven to live with Him. None of my sins were covered by Jesus' blood. The judgment is terrible, terrible!"

"You don't have to worry about God's judgment," Susan began.

"Sure, you aren't worried. You have the robe!" Eric sobbed.

Aunt Myrtle held him close and tried to comfort and soothe his fears. He wouldn't listen to her. "I need the robe!" he cried.

Susan and Aunt Myrtle looked at each other. Then it seemed like a light went on in Aunt Myrtle's eyes. "You mean the white robe of Christ's righteousness?"

"Yes, that's what God said I didn't have."

"You have had a terrible dream, Eric. But I think it's been good. I've wanted to explain that to you several times, but somehow—"

"Just tell me right now," Eric pleaded.

"You're right. There is a judgment time. It's not a time to fear because this is the time when God merely recognizes for the last time if we have chosen Christ as our Saviour or not. He respects our choice. He wants us to choose Him out of love for Him."

Eric shook his head. "But I did choose Him. It wasn't enough."

"When we choose Jesus, we accept His forgiveness for our sins and He covers our sins with His blood. They are forgotten by God."

"That's right," Eric agreed. "Susan's pages were covered by the words *Forgiven by My blood.*"

Susan stared at Eric. She wanted to ask about the book, but Aunt Myrtle continued. "When we accept Jesus, He gives us the robe of righteousness. It's a free gift of His goodness that covers our life. While we wear it, He works to change us so that we are more like Him. But only His goodness stands in the judgment. Our goodness can never save us or make us look good to God."

"But what about all the good things we do?" Eric asked.

"Eric, we obey God and do good because we love Him and want to please Him. It isn't to save ourselves or to be proud about. It's because we love Him so. He actually makes it possible for us to do anything good. We're helpless on our own."

Eric let the words sink into his troubled mind. No wonder Susan always felt so happy. She had the robe. He could have it too. Free! Fear evaporated in him like the dew when the golden sun shines above the horizon. He sighed.

"We can talk about this more tomorrow." Aunt Myrtle yawned. "I'm glad you had the dream."

25

Threads of Love

"What's wrong with Aunt Myrtle?" Susan whispered to Eric as they dusted off the assortment of bottles that cluttered the shelves of Dr. Foster's examining room.

"I don't know," Eric answered. "Yesterday I saw her staring out the window in my room. When she caught me watching her, she jumped a mile high, then got busy smoothing out my bedcovers."

"You should have seen her this morning when Dr. Foster came to pick us up. Her face looked as cloudy as this murky stuff." Susan held up a bottle of gray liquid labeled Poison.

"Everybody sure is grouchy these days," Eric agreed. "Dr. Foster hasn't teased us once. He just stays in his office."

"Grown-ups sure are funny," Susan decided, shaking her head.

The twins let silence fill the room as they buffed the stainless steel examining table until they could see their faces reflected on its surface.

"I'm coming over to talk this out, Myrtle," Dr. Foster's voice rang out. "You're just in love with an old dream, and it's about to become a real nightmare." *Slam*. The twins heard the telephone receiver clatter into its place and a chair crash against the wall. Dr. Foster's office door opened with a bang. He slammed it behind him, then stood there, staring at the twins as though seeing them for the first time that day.

"Come on," Dr. Foster commanded. "We have more important work than this to do."

Eric and Susan dropped their dustcloths, followed Dr. Foster to the Jeep, and climbed into the back seat.

"I tell you," Dr. Foster shouted to no one in particular, "a woman doesn't know her own mind."

"What does that mean?" Susan blurted from the back seat.

"It means, Susan, that your Aunt Myrtle is about to marry a man who can't make her happy because he doesn't love her or anything that is important to her."

The twins exchanged startled glances.

"From the very day she agreed to marry your father, she has been cross, and the light has gone out of her eyes," Dr. Foster continued.

"It's true," Eric whispered to Susan. "I bet Aunt Myrtle is in love with Dr. Foster and doesn't know it."

"Why, of all things!" Susan wailed. "Don't you want her to marry Dad so we can all be together?"

"I thought I did," Eric whispered, "but it isn't going to work. Dad has changed an awful lot. He loves his work about as much as anything. Being a prosecuting lawyer is tough. I don't think Dad cares much about anything else."

"I've just got to talk some sense into that woman!" The Jeep skidded to a stop in Aunt Myrtle's driveway, and Dr. Foster jumped out, slamming the door so hard that Susan and Eric winced.

Dr. Foster stomped toward the kitchen door, then suddenly stopped. There stood Aunt Myrtle in the flower garden. She wore the same pink flowered dress that Eric remembered from the first day he and Susan had met her at the airport. A pair of clippers dangled from one hand, and over her other arm hung a large basket of roses. A gust of wind caught her brown curls and tossed them about beneath her straw hat. It swirled her fluffy dress. When she looked up at Dr. Foster, Susan and Eric could not read the message in her eyes.

Dr. Foster just stood there, looking at Aunt Myrtle.

"He's going to tell it to her this time," Eric whispered.

"Oh, no, he isn't!" Susan giggled.

At that moment, Dr. Foster grabbed Aunt Myrtle, swinging her around. He spoke in gentle words. "The very best argument that I have, Myrtle, is that I love you, and I need you here with me by the sea. I know I can make you happy."

He reached up and removed her straw hat, tossing it into the flower bed. Then he kissed her soundly.

"Oh, boy, now comes the mushy stuff," Eric groaned. "Let's get out of here." He poked Susan and grinned.

The twins opened the door and eased out of the Jeep. They sneaked around the house and down to the beach.

"Do you think they will get things worked out?" Susan asked anxiously. She felt bewildered at the sudden change of events.

"Sure," Eric laughed. "And everything is going to be a lot better around here."

"But . . . if she marries Dr. Foster and not Dad, what will happen to us?" Tears began to form in tiny pools in Susan's eyes. They spilled over her cheeks and dropped onto the warm sand.

"I—I don't know. I guess I didn't think about that." Eric fidgeted in the sand beside Susan. "Anyway, crying isn't going to help much." He handed Susan a rumpled tissue from his shirt pocket.

"I'm sorry," Susan sniffed. "Everything seems so mixed up around here."

"Not everything," Eric encouraged. "At least I understand how to be a Christian. When you and Aunt Myrtle explained about the robe of Jesus' righteousness, it was like a key that unlocked my confused brain. Thanks for helping me, Susan." He patted Susan's shoulder.

"Besides, I think God has a plan," Eric said after they had sat in silence a long time.

"A plan?" Susan asked, drying her tears.

"Sure." Eric grinned. "Come on! Let's go for a walk, and I'll tell you."

Susan and Eric followed the scalloped watermarks along the sand until the brown rocks and tide pools.

Eric stopped and leaned over. "Hey, Susan, look! That's one of the biggest mussel shells I've ever seen." He pointed at a mass of pear-shaped shells that clung to the rocks just above the water. "I'll get it for you."

Eric edged his way over the rough rocks. He reached out to grasp the shell, and a wave slapped against the rocks, sending up a fine spray. He screamed and jumped back. "I'll get it this time," he assured Susan, who stood giggling at his antics.

Eric bent down and tugged at the mussel. He twisted and groaned and pulled. Another wave smashed against the mussel shell bed and soaked Eric. His hair dripped salt water into his eyes and down his neck.

"I need a knife," he decided. "There seem to be tough white threads holding those mussels onto the rocks."

"Those are the byssus threads, Eric."

"They sure are strong."

"It's a good thing. Look at those waves!" Susan pointed. "A mussel lives in a dangerous place. Those threads just hold it neatly to the rocks."

"That's just what I meant to tell you," Eric said. "God's love is stronger than those byssus threads. He cares for us. He has plans for us."

"I suppose you're right," Susan agreed. "Just last week Dr. Foster said the same thing. God even plans the way this world will end. When He comes again everything will happen according to plan."

"You see?" Eric said happily. "I like the idea that we will live in heaven for 1,000 years while the wicked are dead and Satan has no one to confuse anymore."

Susan hugged herself. "Me too. I like the description of the beautiful New Jerusalem in Revelation 21. To think we will come down to earth again in that beautiful city."

"It's going to be a good day when all the wicked, and especially old Satan, are burned up," Eric said. "Then Jesus will make this sad old world all new."

"I do wish everyone would learn about God's plan and choose Him," Susan said wistfully. She looked at Eric. "Let's go home now."

Home! Eric thought. *I wonder just where home will be now.* He knew in his heart that Dad didn't really want two teenagers to put up with when his work demanded all his time. If Aunt Myrtle married Dr. Foster, where would he and Susan go? He didn't say a word to Susan about his doubts. They trudged silently toward the house, each busy with their own thoughts.

"Susan," Eric said at last, "don't forget God is a God of good plans. He will care for us. Besides, we have each other."

"I know, Eric. I know you will take care of me, I . . ."

"Look!" Eric exclaimed, pointing. "There are Aunt Myrtle and Dr. Foster coming down the beach!"

26

Unlocked at Last

A re you sure this is what you two want to do?" Dr. Foster and the twins stood around the pile of luggage in the bustling airport. "We haven't really talked this out."

"Yeah," Eric mumbled in an unconvincing voice. "We just think it's best to be with Dad now."

"You know that we love you," Aunt Myrtle said, clutching Dr. Foster's hand. She brushed a stray tear from her eye.

"Now, Myrtle," Dr. Foster said. "We don't own these young people. If they feel they should go east—"

Eric winced when he realized Dr. Foster couldn't finish the sentence. The crowded room buzzed with the clatter of jumbled noises. A child cried in the distance. Susan wanted to cry, but she pressed her lips together and squinted to hold back the tears. Eric fidgeted with his camera case. He thought the waiting would never end and then feared that it suddenly would.

Two weeks had passed since Aunt Myrtle and Dr. Foster ran over the warm sand, laughing and shouting the good news. They would be married in a month. Eric and Susan felt so happy for them, yet they didn't know what to do. Surely there wouldn't be room in their life for two kids. They'd finally decided to go live with Dad.

"Flight 672 now boarding for Washington, D.C.," a voice boomed over the PA system.

Eric saw Aunt Myrtle stiffen and tighten her grasp on Dr. Foster's hand. Somehow he knew he'd made the wrong decision.

"You don't have to—" Aunt Myrtle started. She noticed Dr. Foster's frown and stopped. "Be careful," she said.

Susan wanted to scream. She looked at Eric. He had locked all his feelings inside himself, just like the day Mother died. Susan felt torn from the one place of security she'd known since that day. But somehow Eric couldn't be left to go off alone.

"We're going to be OK," Susan heard herself stammer. "Don't worry." She kissed Aunt Myrtle on the cheek and ran after Eric, who'd already started down the ramp.

"You know where home is," Dr. Foster called after her.

You know where home is! You know where home is! Dr. Foster's words tumbled over and over in her mind during the next three weeks. School would soon start. Life must go on. But the whole problem was she *didn't* know where home was.

"I'm so miserable," she moaned to Eric one evening after Dad had left them alone again. "I've tried to talk to Dad about our new life and to be patient with that woman he brings home."

"I know," Eric agreed. "If she says once more, 'Oh, aren't you just a little darling,' I'll scream."

"I just hate the thin, hollow way she laughs, and she looks more like a scarecrow decorated up for Christmas than a woman." Susan started to sob. "Oh, I shouldn't talk like this, but you don't think Dad would marry her, do you?"

The question hung over them like a great black cloud.

They sat in silence, each trying to untangle the thoughts that swirled about inside their minds.

"Eric, let's go back!" Susan blurted out suddenly. "It's driving Dad nuts to have us here. We can't seem to reach him."

"I don't know what to do," Eric admitted. "I overheard them talking last night. She begged Dad to send us off to a military boarding school or something."

"Why, that—" Susan caught herself and stuffed the ugly words down inside with the other lonely, sad words that she didn't want to say out loud. She picked up her Bible and flipped the pages.

"I guess no one wants us," Eric mumbled. He let his blond head fall onto his folded arms and sat hunched up on the floor.

"God does!" Susan heard herself say. "And heaven is our home."

"What?" Eric asked in surprise. He noticed a new, determined look on Susan's tearstained face.

"Look at this!" Susan shouted. She held up her Bible. The pages were open to John 14.

"In My Father's house are many dwelling places; if it were not so, I would have told you; for I go to prepare a place for you. And if I go and prepare a place for you, I will come again, and receive you to Myself; that where I am, there you may be also" (verses 2, 3, NASB).

Eric stared at the words. There was a God who was preparing a home for them right now. Surely this same God knew their trouble. He would know what they should do. Why hadn't Eric remembered to pray sooner?

"Susan," he said in a strong voice, "we may not be at home here, and we can't stay with Aunt Myrtle, but we are going to ask God what to do right now."

After they each prayed and poured out their troubles

to God, Eric said firmly, "Susan, we're going back to Aunt Myrtle. She'll know how to help us. I should have talked with her and Dr. Foster before flipping out like this. I'm sorry."

Susan's pursed mouth changed into a delighted smile. "I think you're right. God must know where we can camp for a while until He comes again."

"You're crazy, Susan," Eric laughed. "But I'm glad. It felt good to laugh."

Two days later the arrangements had been made for tickets, and Dad had given them permission to leave. After the long flight a cab dropped the twins off at Aunt Myrtle's house.

"Boy, this feels good!" Susan shouted as she scrambled up the familiar steps to their rooms. She stopped suddenly at the top of the stairs and gasped. In place of Eric's small room stood the open framework of a large unfinished room. It looked like an ugly skeleton mocking her.

"Eric," Susan shouted, "your room! It's gone! Gone!"

She turned to open the door of her room, fearing some terrible thing she couldn't label. The door burst open with a bang. No fluffy curtains greeted her. No soft bed welcomed her to rest. Instead, she looked at a large desk, several chairs, and a wall of bookcases crammed with endless books.

"Oh, Eric," she wailed, and slumped onto the carpeted stairs.

Eric pushed past her and stared at the scene. Any trace that they had belonged here had been erased. So they weren't wanted here, either! He slumped beside Susan. All hope seemed gone.

"Wait a minute! Here we go again. We're going to stop right now and ask God what to do. He'll help us. I know it." Eric wiped his freckled face with one hand.

". . . and we can't stay here, either. They've torn out our rooms. What do You want us to do? We know You love us," Eric prayed.

After the prayer they sat tearfully on the steps. *If I'm ever going to trust God's love for me, this is the time,* Eric thought to himself. Neither of them moved. They didn't know what to do next.

"Someone is in the house," Aunt Myrtle said, entering the back door. Suddenly she caught sight of the twins huddled at the top of the steps. "You've come home!" she shouted in surprise. "Merle, come quick!" Aunt Myrtle dashed up the stairs.

She grabbed the twins and nearly dragged them down the stairs in her excitement. "Come and see," she chattered.

They walked through the living room and entered a short new hallway. Dr. Foster caught up with them as they stood staring at two open doors.

"Go on, look inside," Aunt Myrtle commanded.

The twins disappeared inside the rooms Aunt Myrtle pointed out so excitedly.

"My curtains . . . and bed . . . Oh!" Eric heard Susan shout.

He stared at his room, trying to see everything at once. There stood his surfboard. It had been too large to take east. The room shouted welcome. It contained everything he loved. Eric ran to Susan's room. She stood gazing past her fluffy curtains into the flower garden.

"Is this real?" she squealed.

"I think so," he stammered.

"Welcome home!" Aunt Myrtle's laugh filled every empty space inside Susan.

Dr. Foster flashed them his famous grin. "Welcome home!"

Eric thought they must be the two most wonderful words in the whole world. Then he remembered three other words that he wanted to say. He wanted to say them often the rest of his life. He felt a key turn inside his locked heart and gently open the door. He realized that at last he trusted, and trust had won. The door to his heart opened wide. Fear and confusion about his future and about life fled. The shining key of love had opened his locked-up heart.

All at once the four of them tumbled together, laughing and crying.

"It's good to be home," Eric said in a very grown-up voice. "I love you all so much."

Susan stared at Eric. He didn't look embarrassed at all. She saw the joy and peace in his eyes. His sad heart had opened at last.

Kids' books with kick!

Thunder, the Maverick Mustang, by Nora Ann Kuehn.

Ken and his brother Bob worked hard on old man Weese's ranch to earn the black mustang. Ken loved the fiery pony with all his heart, but Thunder refused to be tamed. Ken was stubborn too. He would win the pony's affections with kindness, no matter what.

Just when Thunder begins to calm down, a forest fire burns the fence posts, and he escapes. Is Ken's love strong enough to make the black mustang come home?

US$6.95/Cdn$8.70. Paper, 96 pages.

The Fiery Dragon Gang, by Ginger Ketting.

Secret passwords. Mysterious adventures. Hidden clubhouses. An enemy to spy on. These are the ingredients to a recipe for fun with the kids of *The Fiery Dragon Gang*.

Five friends start the club to have a good time, but things soon get out of hand when they start leaving Jerry out of the fun.

When two new kids show up, the tables are turned, and Addie learns a lesson she'll never forget.

US$7.95/Cdn$9.95. Paper, 128 pages.

Please photocopy and complete the form below.

- -

❑ *Thunder, the Maverick Mustang*

US$6.95/Cdn$8.70.

❑ *The Fiery Dragon Gang*

US$7.95/Cdn$9.95.

Please add applicable sales tax and 15% (US$2.50 minimum) to cover postage and handling.

Name _____

Address _____

City _____

State _____ Zip _____

Price	$ _____	Order from your Adventist Book Center or ABC
Postage	$ _____	Mailing Service, P.O. Box 7000, Boise, Idaho
Sales Tax	$ _____	83707. Prices subject to change without notice.
TOTAL	$ _____	Make check payable to Adventist Book Center.

© 1990 Pacific Press Publishing Association 2233